The Consorts

MELISSA ADDEY

THE CONSORTS

Copyright © 2016 by Melissa Addey. All rights reserved.

First Paperback Print Edition: 2016 in United Kingdom

The moral right of the author has been asserted.

Published by Letterpress Publishing
Cover and Formatting: Streetlight Graphics

Paperback ISBN: 978-1-910940-09-9

No part of this book may be reproduced, scanned, or distributed in any printed or electronic form without permission. Please do not participate in or encourage piracy of copyrighted materials in violation of the author's rights. Thank you for respecting the hard work of this author.

For my own little prince, Seth

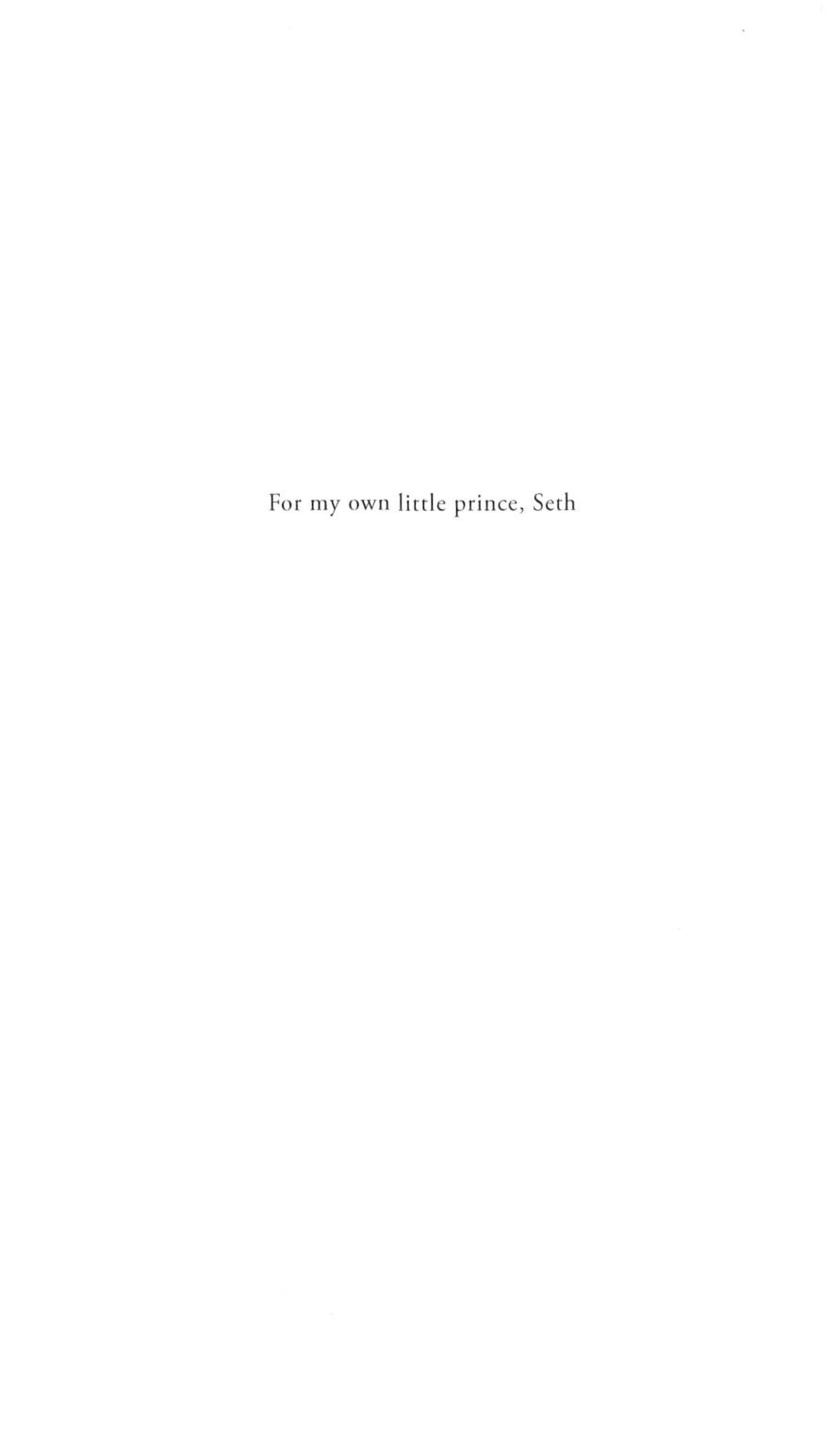

A full-length novel set in the Forbidden City of the 1700s, ***The Fragrant Concubine*** is based on the true story of a Muslim woman sent from a conquered land to be the Emperor's new concubine and the many legends that grew up around her.

The Historical Novel Society's Editor's Choice: *I enjoyed the human drama, the love and hurt, the scheming for revenge, rivalries and loyalties in the Forbidden City. Reading this novel was a moving and wonderful excursion into a different time.*

Spelling and Pronunciation

I have used the international Pinyin system for the Chinese names of people and places. The following list indicates the elements of this spelling system that may cause English speakers problems of pronunciation. To the left, the letter used in the text, to the right, its equivalent English sound.

The Empress' name, Lady Fuca, is pronounced Foo-cha.

c	=	ts
q	=	ch
x	=	sh
z	=	dz
zh	=	j

The Forbidden City, China, 1700s

Honoured Ladies

BAO IS FUSSING. "PERHAPS THE pink is better," he worries, lifting first one and then another flower to my already laden headdress and frowning at both. First attendant amongst my eunuchs and maids, head of my household, Bao is always worrying about something.

I sigh. "Bao, what does it matter?"

"It *matters*," insists Bao. "It always matters when the new ladies are brought into the Forbidden City. The Emperor may be taken with their novelty, but he must not forget the ladies who already reside here."

I make a face at him in the mirror of my dressing table. "The Emperor is besotted with Empress Fuca as well you know," I point out. "He barely notices the rest of us." This is true, although I also know that I too readily use this truth to mask my own failures.

Bao is not put off so easily. "The Empress is a wonderful woman," he says dutifully, "but the Emperor is still young and a young man has need of variety. He will come to call upon his other ladies more often, you will see. And when he does, he needs to remember your face."

I look into the mirror before me while Bao concedes to the last of the early spring's pink camellias and busies himself tucking them securely into my hair, fastening them with jade pins and rearranging multiple strands of pearls to his satisfaction.

"And think," says Bao, stepping back and regarding his handiwork with a beaming smile, "If His Majesty should look upon you with favour then you might have a child. Such a blessing."

I've heard this too often, though I know loyal Bao means well. I would like a child of my own, to share my life here, but I doubt it will ever happen.

In the mirror I see a young woman's face. A pretty face, certainly after Bao's careful ministrations. An elegant face, of course, for the Honoured Ladies of my rank are always elegant in their grooming.

A lonely face.

My palanquin bobs its way through the tiny passageways of the Inner Court. We pass by many other small palaces, each close to the next, separated only by their gardens. Here reside all the women of the court. We are a world of women, children, maids and eunuchs. Amongst our femininity towers the palace of the Emperor himself, the only man allowed to reside in the Forbidden City.

There is a change in our pace as we come through the gates to the Outer Court, the public face of our lives. Here are mighty temples and receiving halls, watchtowers and endless courtyards, golden lions guarding marble plinths. Everywhere there are scurrying or imposing officials of varying ranks, armoured guards, colourful flags, noise. I let the curtains of my palanquin drop. I am unused to all of this. I hardly ever venture into the Outer Court except for the greatest of occasions.

We arrive at the grand receiving hall and I join the other ladies of the court there. Most I know only at a distance. I begin by making my obeisance to the Empress Fuca. She's older than me and is known as a kindly womanbut she is so exalted that I see little of her. Still, she inclines her head and smiles when I bow to her. She was only sixteen when she married the Emperor and although it was an arranged marriage, still Heaven must have smiled on their union, for the two young people fell in love and have remained devoted ever since. There are many other women here at court but few have had much opportunity of advancing, since the Emperor's affections lie so firmly with his Empress. Other ladies are called to his chambers from time to time, but not as often as any of them would like and so very few have risen through the ranks. Amongst our numbers there are only two women whom everyone knows and watches, for it is clear that they are the most ambitious amongst us. I look about me and quickly spot them.

Lady Ling was only a lady-in-waiting, not even a chosen concubine, when I first came here but two years ago she caught the Emperor's eye and within a year had been promoted twice – first to an Honoured Lady like myself, then to an Imperial Concubine. I am not sure what she has done to be so liked, for she has not yet born a son, only a daughter. Whispers wondered if, being Han Chinese, she offered variety from many of the other ladies who are Manchus, but I am Han by birth myself and it has not made me a favourite. The whispers went on to suggest that she must therefore be very accomplished in the bedchamber and those who whisper watch her to see how high she can rise on such skills alone. Today she stands with her head held high, her body held erect, full of confidence. Her robes are a rich purple with complex embroidery and her hair is full of silken flowers.

The other woman whom all the court knows is Lady Ula Nara. Already a Noble Consort, only two ranks lower than the Empress herself, Ula Nara has been at court since before the Emperor was enthroned. There are others more senior to her, but Ula Nara is known to be a jealous woman. She craves the position of Empress, though that is unlikely to ever happen, for Empress Fuca has been the Emperor's Primary Consort since he was a prince and he did not hesitate to make her Empress once he ascended the throne. Today Ula Nara is in full court dress, her robes a rich yellow: not quite the imperial yellow to which she aspires, but certainly close to it. Her posture is immaculate but there is a tension in how she holds herself that speaks of something hidden below, a fear or even an anger, it is hard to tell. Her hair glitters with gems. Ula Nara is fond of jewellery.

We have gathered to mark the end of the Daughters' Draft, the lengthy selection process for new concubines, when every Manchu girl between thirteen and sixteen must be presented at court so that the Emperor may have his pick of them. Today those chosen will enter the Forbidden City and join our ranks. This is a day when the ambitious and the jealous are watchful and afraid. They scan the new faces for future rivals. The rest of us wonder what use the Emperor can have for more women when he makes little use of the ones he already has.

I find a space to stand but as other ladies arrive after me I find myself edged forwards until, to my dismay, I am side by side with Lady Ula Nara. I keep my eyes low so as not to meet her gaze and try not to move too much, so that I will not draw her attention to me. But perhaps I need not worry. Ula Nara's face is tight with tension, her eyes are locked firmly onto the great doors through which will enter first the Emperor and then each of the new arrivals.

There is much rustling and jostling for a good viewing position before a loud call announces the Emperor and we all fall to our knees to complete the sequence of kowtows required as he strides past and takes up his place on the imperial throne. By his side is the Empress Dowager, his mother, who gives him a brief smile before nodding to the Chief Eunuch to begin the naming of the girls who are about to become concubines. In theory it is the Emperor's mother who chooses each girl. In practice the choices have mostly been made through the endless checks that are made into everything from each girl's lineage and family to her body odour, height, quality of hair and demeanour. Any found wanting will have been sent away long before now. Any actual choosing the Empress Dowager has done was from a bevy of already-perfect beauties.

The Consorts

The naming goes on for a long time, tedious in its elaborate detail. Each girl advances, kowtows, has her family announced before being given a new name which wipes out her past and brings her like a fresh empty scroll to our world, ready to have a new destiny written upon it. There are not even that many new women this year but the proclamations are so slow there might as well be hundreds. Endless titles and allocations of silver, jewels, servants and palaces are read out for each new face. I shift in boredom and stifle a yawn. To amuse myself I do not look at any of the new girls until I have guessed by the look on Ula Nara's face how beautiful each one is. I almost laugh when her face darkens in rage and I turn to see a very beautiful girl join us. The more senior ranks are called first, before we slowly work downwards.

We have reached the Honoured Ladies, my own rank: higher than a lady in waiting but not by much. A few girls are named and enter our strange lives. I'm surprised as Ula Nara's face lightens with relief and I turn to see what manner of ugly girl has somehow slipped through the rigorous selection process.

She is not Manchu, nor Chinese. She is a Mongol, something of a rarity amongst us, with high broad cheekbones and very white skin. Her cheeks are painted pink, for the Mongols prize pink cheeks on their pale-skinned women. She seems older than many of the girls, at least sixteen and perhaps closer to seventeen. They have taken away her own traditional clothes and dressed her in the Manchu style. She will have been used to striding about in sturdy boots and now she must sway precariously on our cloud-climbing shoes, raised a full hand's width above the ground on a tiny platform requiring a good deal of practice to walk in. Her black hair has been pinned with the first white almond blossoms and she is tall, taller than many of the women here. Her eyes are dark and I think at once of a hawk or falcon, perhaps even a young eagle such as the Mongols use for hunting. Fettered by her high shoes, the heavy silken robes, her almond blossom hair, but fierce and longing to be free. This is no dainty girl who will fly to the Emperor's command. This is a wild bird. No wonder Ula Nara is relieved. She is not ugly, but no-one could imagine this girl trying hard to please the Emperor, simpering and longing for his attention. I will be surprised if she does not die here, fading away as wild birds often do if you try to cage them.

"Honoured Lady Ying," announces the Chief Eunuch and I stifle a laugh. Her new name denotes intelligence but also brings to mind the eagle. She has been well named. She looks about her, twisting her neck and shifting uneasily on her cloud-climbing shoes. As she is led past us to leave the ceremony she stumbles and a eunuch has to catch her before she falls. She stands again, flustered and angry at her loss of dignity. I smile at her, wanting to reassure her and she gives me a small tight smile in return, unsure of my intentions.

"I am Qing," I tell her before she has a chance to move away, hardly even knowing why I am addressing her. "Welcome to court," I add, almost blurting out the words.

She hovers, uncertain whether to follow the gesturing eunuch or speak with me.

"I'd follow the eunuch, if I were you."

I startle. Lady Ula Nara has been watching us and now she has intervened. I bow my head to her and Lady Ying awkwardly follows suit.

"You are new to court," says Ula Nara, speaking only to Ying and ignoring me. "You cannot be expected to know with whom you should associate. But I would suggest that you do not waste your time on those who may bring you ill luck through being supremely ill favoured." As she finishes speaking she sinks into a gracious bow to the Emperor and leaves the hall.

I stand still in front of the new arrival. I can feel heat rising up my neck and know that an ugly blotchy stain is creeping from my collarbones up into my face. I know now why I spoke to her: because I hoped that an outsider would not know what there is to know about me, that someone here might overlook my failings. I struggle to meet the curious gaze of the newcomer before she is hurried away by her guide.

Somehow I make my way from the hall and back into my palanquin, where I have a few moments of solitude to force the rising tears out of my eyes and to cool the flush of shame that has scarred me. Bao waits in my courtyard garden, eager for gossip.

"Well?" he asks before I've even alighted from my chair.

"The usual," I say. "Mostly pretty, one very beautiful that annoyed Lady Ula Nara." I pause, thinking of angry eyes under delicate almond blossom, of my crushing shame at Ula Nara's words. "And a Lady Ying," I say, despite myself.

"Who, my Lady?"

I don't even know why I said her name. I don't want to tell my loyal Bao what Ula Nara said. I have heard it too many times before from other lips and he will only hurry to reassure me, to comfort me that her truthful words were false. I shrug. "She looked cross," I say. I don't want to tell Bao that she was like a fettered eagle. He will think I have gone mad.

Bao tuts. "What has she to be cross about?" he says. "She has been chosen as a concubine for the Son of Heaven. What more could a woman wish for?"

"A glimpse of him from time to time?" I say.

Spring passes away and as the weather grows warm we move from the high red walls of the Forbidden City into the open green spaces and wide lakes of the Summer Palace. On our first day there I set out early to walk alone along the lakeside, one of my favourite pastimes.

"You spend too much time alone," sighs Bao. "You should at least walk with one of the other ladies to pick fruit or flowers. I can send a maid with you to carry baskets if you need one. Or go down to the lake house where they play card games. Why don't you spend time with the ladies there? Some are quite pleasant, I'm sure."

I shake my head. "I'm happy alone," I say with a bright smile. Bao lets me go, but not before he lets his hand rest on my head a little longer than is necessary to check my hairpins are in place and I hear him murmur a blessing for me under his breath. I leave quickly so that he will not see the sudden welling up of tears in my eyes. Bao is like a father to me but I never tell him that I am not brave enough to bear the whispers of the ladies when I draw close. What Ula Nara spoke out loud, they only mutter to one another. I would rather be lonely than ashamed.

There's a violent splashing nearby and I turn to see what is causing it. A boat is drifting on the lake, its sole occupant a concubine who is trying to master the oars. She pulls hard on one side and the boat twists round rather than gliding forward, the lesser-used oar crashing into the water so that her silken robe is splashed. She tries again and this time the boat swings the other way, turning towards me, so that she finds herself back where she was before and splashed once again. I recognise the newcomer, Lady Ying, her pale skin now pink-cheeked through her efforts alone. She is enraged.

"You stupid, stupid... useless *thing*!" she yells, her voice far louder than any lady's should ever be. She jerks at the oar, which has now become stuck in the watery depths, perhaps entangled in the lotus roots below. Her face contorts with anger and effort.

I can't help it, I laugh out loud. She is so angry, so much how I remember my first glimpse of her. Several months in our gilded cage have not tamed this eagle.

She hears me and looks up, her boat by now close to the shore. At the sight of me she tries to stand up, using one oar as a support. "Help me out of this ridiculous thing," she calls.

I start towards her but she has already pushed too hard on the oar, trying to move the boat closer to me, and the boat comes forward faster than she expected, the oar pulling her arm, unbalancing her altogether. There is a moment when she tries and fails to regain her footing and then she is in the water, spluttering and gasping. I run to her and kneel, holding out my hand from the very edge of the lake and grasping her as she reaches for me. Our hands interlock and I am conscious, for a brief moment, of the warmth from her tight grip. It is an effort to pull her out but I manage it somehow and in a few moments she stands before me, her sky blue robe now soaked to a murky grey, waterweeds clinging to her delicately embroidered silk sleeves. Her hair had been decorated with the first peonies of summer in rosy pinks but now they look bedraggled. We stand for a moment, staring at each other before she speaks.

"Thank you," she manages, in an effort at politeness, before turning to look at the boat, now drifting out of reach. "Wretched thing," she bursts out. "Now it's lost!"

"The eunuchs will bring it back," I tell her, used to having my every need met. I look her over. "You're very wet. Do you want to come to my palace – it is just over there – and have some dry clothes? My first attendant, Bao, will take care of everything."

She nods, chastened a little by her failure. I make my way towards my palace and she follows me, her robes making a stiff wet sound as the soaked silks rub together. "I am Lady Qing," I say to her, the word I use for Lady indicating to her that we are the same rank.

"They have named me Ying," she says by way of introduction.

I nod. "I saw you when you arrived," I say. I do not know if she remembers me from the day when she arrived here. I am not sure I want her to.

But she is looking away from me, across the lakes and I think that on the day she arrived she saw nobody and heard nothing, wrapped up in her own fears as each of us was when we first came here. "I didn't think I would be chosen," she says. "Not many Mongol girls are. I thought I was too tall – the other girls all looked tiny." She is quiet for a few moments. "But here I am," she says finally and her voice is flat.

Bao is appalled. A dripping wet concubine bedecked with waterweeds is a sight he has probably never encountered in his many years of service and he calls for every servant I have to help him. She is led away to my bathroom to be washed with warm water before she catches a chill. Servants are sent running to her own palace to collect dry clothes and inform her household of what has befallen their mistress.

"So careless," opines Bao, as he directs maids to fetch hot tea and little cakes, while calling for another eunuch to ensure Lady Ying's hair is properly reassembled. "Really, they should be whipped, letting their mistress go off alone. Why, anything could happen."

"I walk alone," I say.

"And I watch you from the palace to be sure nothing happens to you," retorts Bao. "She could have drowned. Why wasn't a eunuch rowing the boat for her? A lady has no need to row."

We are interrupted. Freshly dressed in a pale pink robe with tiny rosebuds from my gardens nestled in her hair, Lady Ying now seems younger and less sure of herself, hovering in the doorway. Bao excuses himself.

"Come and have tea," I offer.

She sits opposite me, takes up a small bowl of tea and sips it uncertainly. "Thank you again," she says. "You've been very kind."

"It's nothing," I say and then can't help laughing. "You've been my entertainment this morning."

She smiles, rueful. "They said a eunuch should row me. But I wanted to do it myself, like riding a horse. Only a baby would ride on a horse with someone else holding the reins," she says, some of her fierceness returning.

I think of her home in Mongolia, where they say they have fearsome warrior queens and endless flat grasslands where they can ride at full gallop. "Do you miss your home?" I ask.

She shrugs. "I will never return there, so it's as well not to think of it," she says as though repeating something she was told when parting from her family. Her tone is still fierce but her lower lip trembles.

I try to change the subject. "Perhaps we can go boating together," I find myself offering, although I have never rowed in my life and can only picture Bao's face at the thought. "It might be easier to row with two of us?"

She brightens at once. "Yes," she says. "I would like that." She looks about the room and then at me. "How long have you been at court?" she asks.

"Seven years," I say.

She nods. "Do you see the Emperor often? I mean as a companion," she adds, a small blush rising on her neck.

"Not often," I say.

"How often, though?" she asks, too new to this world to have caught my tone.

Something in me wants to tell her the truth. "Three times," I say.

"A month?" she asks, no doubt thinking this to be quite a lot considering how many women the Emperor may command to his rooms.

"In seven years," I say and see her eyes widen at the reality of her possible future here.

Only a few days passed before I emerged from my bedroom to find Lady Ying waiting for me, Bao providing her with tea but no doubt taken aback by the earliness of the hour and the boldness of a visit that was not even arranged. She waited impatiently while I got dressed – "Why bother with all that decoration in her hair if the Emperor's not going to see her?" she threw at the horrified Bao – and then all but dragged me to the lakeshore. Since then she has arrived every day and every day we flounder on the lake. When we pay attention our rowing improves, but Ying spends most of her time quizzing me about the new world she has joined, which means she does not look at what she is doing and I get distracted.

"But he can't *only* call on the Empress," she protests one day. "Otherwise what is the point of all of us other ladies?"

"Please will you pay attention to the rowing and stop talking about the Emperor?" I ask her, struggling with my own oar while hers trails uselessly in the water.

"So who else does he call on?" she persists.

I sigh and sit back, loosely holding the oar and abandoning any pretence at rowing for the day. "There's a Lady Ling," I offer.

"Who is she?"

"A nobody," I say. "She was just a lady in waiting, there are hundreds of them. She managed to catch the Emperor's eye and got promoted twice inside of a year, first to an Honoured Lady like us, then an Imperial Concubine."

"Children?" asks Ying.

I shake my head. "Only a girl."

"Can't be long till she has a son, if she's a favourite."

I shrug.

"Any other ladies in favour?"

I screw up my nose. "Not really. He and Empress Fuca really do love one another, everyone says she was the perfect match for him. He likes Lady Ling. There's Noble Consort Ula Nara – she's very highly ranked and desperate for his favour but he doesn't seem keen on her.

The Consorts

She's very jealous, she's always throwing tantrums because of other women and he finds it annoying. She goes creeping round the place spying on the other ladies and trying to find faults with them that might get them demoted. You need to keep clear of her, she'll make things up that aren't even true if she can't find any real faults."

"Why?"

I shrug. "She was in love with a man before she was chosen as concubine," I say. "She wouldn't let go of the idea of him. It turned her bitter. She wants everyone to be as unhappy here as she is and she's spent so much time spying and making accusations that now I think she finds pleasure in making other people suffer."

Ying throws scraps of cakes to the ever-eager fish below the boat and sighs. "Do you mean to tell me I'm going to spend the rest of my life here and never even see him?"

"You might," I say. "He might take a liking to you."

"He's never seen me," she scoffs. "I was in a crowd of girls at the selection and in the presentation. I could disappear and he'd know nothing about it."

I laugh. "He would notice a disappearing concubine, even if he didn't know who you were," I say. "Now *row*."

Ying finally sees the Empress up close when we attend a silkworm-raising ceremony. Each of the ladies of the court is required to attend, for silkworms are a precious industry for our empire and the Empress sees it as her duty to request that Heaven looks kindly on it, ensuring that the delicate threads will continue to flow from the tiny corpses into the great looms that provide us with our most prized fabric. The ceremony involves much in the way of mulberry leaves being personally offered to the silkworms by the Empress and all of us ladies with our own hands, as well as many prayers.

"She's not as stuffy as I expected her to be," acknowledges Ying as we are finishing. She's right. Empress Fuca does not over-dress in jewels and imperial yellow. Today she wears a delicate blue robe embroidered with a mulberry design and her hair is bound with summer meadow-flowers rather than the formal headdresses to which she might lay claim.

"And now that we have finished our honours to the gods it is time for us to eat the fruits of this great tree," she says, laughing and waves us towards great platters heaped with ripe mulberries, their flesh sweet and juicy, so that the ladies cluster around, laughing and chattering more freely than usual. The Empress moves amongst us, smiling and speaking easily with each woman, although we can see that her conversation with Ula Nara is brief and the one with Lady Ling briefer still.

"How must it feel to know that everyone wants your throne?" murmurs Ying.

I shrug. "No-one will be getting it any time soon," I say. "So she can be light-hearted."

This year the summer days seem to pass more quickly with Ying at my side. Instead of hours of tedium, pacing by the lakeshores alone, now I have all manner of diversions. We play card games and drinking games and attend ceremonies and rituals that I used to find tedious with no-one to talk to. Ying gives me a puppy, a foolish lolloping thing that has no sense but loves to swim and throws himself into the lakes without a second thought. I name him Fish and swear he has flippers rather than legs. In turn I find her a kitten we name Golden Peach, who seemed fond of caresses at first but slowly turns into a most disdainful animal, preening and posing on the rooftops, soaking up the long summer days into her fur and wholly ignoring us unless we offer titbits. The two creatures keep us busy, either drying the foolish pup or beseeching the cat to grace us with her presence.

The Consorts

We get better at the rowing by the time summer comes to a close, even managing well enough so that we can talk and row at the same time. I take Ying to my favourite parts of the gardens and she terrifies my servants by standing on a swing and swinging so high we are all certain she will fall and harm herself.

"You're a scaredy," she taunts me, flying almost above my head, petals falling from her hair, robes fluttering.

"Yes I am," I call back. "You're mad!"

She forces me to stand on the swing that I have been used to idly sitting and rocking on, one foot safely on the ground. Against Bao's protestations she pushes me until my knuckles are white on the ropes. I feel the terrifying thrill of the ground rushing past me too fast to stop. My mouth opens to protest but I am unable to speak, both for fear and the air that fills my throat. Ying runs from her place behind me so that she can see my face and laughs out loud at my expression, her eyes bright, her pink lips formed into an O mimicking my own. She frowns when she sees my expression suddenly change and turns to see approaching eunuchs. Behind her, I manage to stop the swing and climb down, stumbling then rising dizzily to my feet. I know what this visit means but she does not and I do not know for whom the summons has come.

"Lady Ying?" asks one of the eunuchs.

"Yes?" she says.

"You are the chosen companion for this evening." The eunuchs bow and walk away.

She turns to me. "What do they mean?"

"You've been summoned to the Emperor's bedchamber," I say, blushing a little at having to explain. "You have to tell your first attendant," I say. "He will arrange everything and prepare you. You have to go back to your own palace at once, it'll take all day," I add, vaguely recollecting the last time I was summoned myself.

She stands confused, a little fearful. I try to smile encouragingly and she responds although it's only a half-smile. "Goodbye, then," she offers.

"Goodbye," I say.

She walks away from me and I stand alone but for Bao. He pats my shoulder. "Do not be jealous, my lady," he says. "She is new, he has to call for her at least once. Your time will come again," he adds, staunchly ignoring seven years' worth of evidence to the contrary. "I will prepare you a tea now," he says.

I nod but do not follow him. Instead I stand still, trying to understand the feelings rising up in me. I *am* jealous, but not because of the Emperor's affections. I have no craving for his company, since I barely know him. Instead I find myself angry that he has taken my new friend from me, this wild eagle who has, in one summer, made me laugh more than I have done in the seven years I have spent alone here. He has taken my playmate away so that I have no-one to splash me with muddy lake water and push me too high and too fast on a swing.

I must be going mad. It happens to the women who have been here too long. Most of them end up tending to silkworms as though they were children, or talking all day to their songbirds. The ones who have really gone too far, the ancient concubines of former emperors, live in the most distant palaces and carve gourds into strange misshapen faces.

I must stay away from gourds, I tell myself as the rest of the day passes in a haze of unending boredom, a boredom I foolishly thought had disappeared forever.

A few days pass and I don't see her. Well, it has happened as I expected, I think to myself, kicking a stone as I walk along the lake's edge. She is

The Consorts

gone – sucked into the scheming world of the court women, plotting and planning how each of them may get a little closer to the Emperor, how they may draw attention to themselves and obscure their fellow concubines. Even Ying, who I thought was wild and different and would be hard to tame to this strange world. Even she has succumbed, the fettered bird of prey coming to the call of its master, flying to his hand without question.

More days pass and then Ying appears in my rooms. She is subdued, quiet. She turns down my offers of refreshments and silently shakes her head when I half-heartedly ask if she would like to go rowing. I feel my spirits fall further. It is as I thought. She is gone but has called on me out of a dreary, well-meant politeness, a favourite pitying a nobody.

"May we walk in your gardens?" she asks at last.

I rise. The silence indoors has grown oppressive and at least if we walk I can make meaningless small talk regarding flowers or the weather. I hope she will leave soon and return to her own palace and then leave me alone, as I used to be. No doubt I'll grow used to it again, after all I managed not to carve gourds before.

We walk a little in silence and then sit down beneath a small canopy of flowers, on cushions left there for my comfort. I say nothing about her night with the Emperor (or perhaps there was more than one night, I think sadly. Perhaps she is already a much-desired favourite). It would be unspeakably vulgar to discuss matters of the bedroom so I keep quiet. But now that we are away from the servants Ying regains her voice.

"I doubt he'll call me back again," she blurts out suddenly as we sit in my garden. Her face is turned away from me as she ostentatiously smells some flowers.

I'm desperate to know more, however improper it is to ask. I wait but she is silent. I'm blushing furiously but I have to know. "Why not?" I ask her violet-silk back.

She shrugs, hot colour creeping up her neck as she turns back to face me. "I didn't know what to do," she says. "He had to show me everything I should do and I wasn't very good at it. I think – I think I bit him," she adds in a half-whispered rush, head down.

I gasp back a laugh. "What?"

She's giggling now, looking up at me, her hands covering half her face, only her eyes peeping at me. "I didn't mean to!"

And we're both laughing helplessly, rocking back and forth on the soft cushions until she falls into my lap, her hands pressed over her mouth in a desperate effort to stop. I look down at her wide eyes and feel her whole body shake with her barely suppressed, spluttering giggles. The petals from the late roses in her hair are coming loose and drifting over my robe onto the grass and suddenly I am happy. My days of lonely boredom are over at last. She does not shy away from my bad luck with the Emperor. She has not been stolen away into the scheming world of the other women, as I had feared. She is still here – my only friend – and she is mine.

Empress

THE AUTUMN LEAVES BEGIN TO fall and we are removed from the freedom of our summer home and brought back within the high red walls of the Forbidden City, where the cold winds and hard frosts soon force us to retreat still further until we are trapped indoors. Unable to venture out, there seems to be nothing to do but play board games or drinking games. I quickly tire of both.

As ever it is Ying that changes our routine and Bao that mutters and huffs at her presumption. I am barely even dressed one chilly day, my hair hangs loose and my feet are bare, when there is an unexpected pounding on our door and Ying bursts into my rooms, still in her sleeping robe, her hair loose and ruffled from her bed, cheeks pink from the cold. Our two palaces sit side by side, only a walkway separates them.

"I couldn't bear the thought of a whole morning of dressing alone!" she exclaims. "It takes hours and I get so bored. It will be more fun together!"

Bao's face makes me giggle but I overrule his pleading glance. "Tea for Lady Ying," I instruct a maid, who gawps at the sight of the undressed visitor.

Ying is too clever not to know that it is Bao that must be won over, not I. "Bao, will you oversee my hair too?" she begs. "I had them send over my clothes. You always know what hairstyle should accompany each robe. You have such good taste."

Bao very nearly blushes. "You have no idea how to manage your servants," he says crossly. "You should whip them all for being so lazy. Sit here and I'll pin your hair first. It hasn't even been brushed!"

Ying sits, a picture of meek obedience although her eyes catch mine in the mirror and there is mischief in them.

Now there is a new rhythm to our winter days. Ying takes to her palanquin as soon as she rises from her bed. Still in her night robes, wrapped in blankets to keep her warm, she is carried all of fifty paces to my rooms, a servant trotting alongside to carry her clothes for the day. Once in my palace, she emerges from her silken cocoon and settles herself in my bedroom, where the maids help us both to dress and Bao sees to our hair. We do not rush, for what is there to hurry us? We slurp bowls of hot rice porridge and munch on warm honey buns, sip hot tea and talk endlessly of nothing. We giggle for no reason, while whoever is not being attended to lolls on my bed, night robe and blankets draped carelessly over bare legs and arms. It takes us till the middle of the day to be correctly attired for anyone to see us. We quickly lose any shyness at seeing one another half-dressed, playing silly games of catch around the rooms while the maids giggle at our foolishness and Bao holds his hands up in horror when our hair, only half-pinned, falls back down our backs, gemstones hitting the floor as maids scurry to collect them.

"Why doesn't she just *live* here," Bao grumbles, but after a while he finds out how to prepare Mongolian specialities and has them made for her as a surprise. He keeps stocks of her favourite teas and sweets ready and waiting for her daily visits and is grudgingly proud that she would rather spend her time in my palace – or his household, as he no doubt thinks of it, than her own. She flatters him while he mutters about her being a nuisance to dress. "Always on the move, always giggling and being foolish, leading my mistress astray with your nonsense. She never used to cause me half the trouble *you* do. Be off with you now," he adds, as darkness falls and the lanterns are lit in my courtyard. "Back to your own rooms, shoo. I cannot imagine what your good-for-nothing servants do all day, since you are always here."

Ying only ever laughs at him and waves as she enters her chair. She grins at me before pulling the curtain closed over her tiny palanquin window and I lift my hand to bid her farewell from where I stand inside the doorway of my rooms. Bao drags me away. "Too cold! You will catch your death and I shall be blamed for it, oh yes, it is always the servants that are blamed when their mistresses are so stubborn."

"I miss her when she goes," I say sadly. "My rooms seem empty without her."

"*Miss* her?" echoes Bao. "How can you miss her? You know very well she will be here tomorrow morning before I have even had a chance to have the fires lit. What do you want her to do, stay the night? Sleep in your bed? The two of you are inseparable. At least you are happy now you have a friend," he adds. "Though you don't talk to your poor old Bao any more, oh no. Too busy with your precious Lady Ying to remember your loyal servant."

I laugh and slap away his hands that are held up in mock pity. "You should be pleased," I say. "You used to tell me off for complaining that I was bored."

"Oh heavens yes," agrees Bao. "I can do my work now that I don't have you following me about like a lost puppy. Thank goodness the two of you have each other. It's not as though either of you has the Emperor's eye," he can't help adding.

"No, we don't," I say flatly. "I'm glad you've stopped hoping."

"One should never stop hoping," says Bao piously.

"I can't stay indoors anymore," says Ying early one morning, as soon as she has arrived. "Let's go out."

"Out where?" I ask, looking at the whirling snow that has been falling all morning and the thick drifts that have piled over the plant pots in my courtyard.

"Out!" she laughs. "In the snow. The servants say that the streams have all frozen up and the snow is as high as a man's knees or more."

"You are *not* going out," says Bao. "And that is final. You will catch a chill and die."

But we insist and he has to content himself with our hurried dressing, our half-pinned hair, heaping both of us up with fur-lined robes and boots until we look like bears, before standing at the window wringing his hands to watch us venture into the increasing snowstorm.

It's freezing. I stand on the walkway of my garden, catching my breath at the shock of the cold after my cosy rooms, where *kangs* burn day and night to keep me warm.

"Come!" says Ying, holding out her hand to me. I take it and step gingerly down from my covered walkway onto the cobbles. I sink to my knees at once, my boots making walking hard going.

We teeter along the tiny lanes of the Inner City, breaking off icicles to suck on, giggling when we slip and fall backwards, staggering to pull one another back up. When we come to the gateways leading to the Outer City I hesitate. But Ying, still tugging at icicles behind me, urges me on and I step forwards alone.

I have never seen the Forbidden City like this. The vast public courtyards, usually so busy with officials and servants, palanquins and guards, stand silent and empty. Whiteness is everywhere and the once-golden rooftops now sparkle with icicles, their imperial colour lost to the might of the snow that has drifted down from Heaven.

I'm about to cautiously step out into the vast space when I'm nearly knocked over by a blow to the head and jerk round to see Ying, doubled over with laughter, her hands forming a second snowball to lob at me. But I'm too fast for her, grabbing a handful of snow and throwing it at her, a straight hit to the belly. Soon we are running round the endless snow-filled landscape, hurling snowballs and laughing so hard it hurts. I slip and fall and she holds out a hand to help me up, clasping me to her as I try to stand, unsteady on the icy flagstones beneath my feet.

"What good friends you are," says a low voice.

I turn from Ying's arms to see Ula Nara standing in the gateway between the Inner and Outer Courts, blocking our way back to the safety of our palaces. Dressed all in a dark blue silk, trimmed with thick brown fur, her face white from the cold, she stands, framed by the spent red lanterns and the whiteness all around her, making her seem an even darker figure than she already is.

We manage to bow, feeling the cold seep back into us after our exertions. "Lady Ula Nara," I manage. "Are you well?"

She doesn't move, doesn't respond to our bows although a strange smile curves her lips. "I was told the two of you were friendly," she says. "I did not know you were *such* good friends."

I feel Ying stiffen beside me and her hand slide away from where she was gripping me by the elbow, trying to keep me upright a moment ago. Unsure of what to do or say I remain silent and Ula Nara's smile grows broader. "I'll take that silence as agreement, shall I?" she says. She turns away and is gone in a moment, nothing but whirling snow where she was standing, as though she was a vision, a ghost.

I turn to Ying. "Ignore her," I say.

But Ying's face has lost its happiness. "It is as you said," she replies, her voice devoid of emotion. "She wants to find fault, even if it means braving a snowstorm to do her snooping."

I spread my hands. "What fault could she find?" I ask. "We were having a snow fight! What is wrong with that?" I know, even as I say this, that I am not quite being honest. There is something between us that Ula Nara can sense, something she has seen before I have even given it a name.

Ying looks at me for a moment and then smiles. "It's cold," she says and puts her arm about my shoulders to lead me back inside. "Bao will be beside himself at how long we have stayed out."

The darkest days of winter are upon us and the Empress is closed away from view. Smallpox visited Beijing and made its way inside the Forbidden City. Despite the inoculations practiced so assiduously within the imperial household, her young son has died. He was her second son to die young and she has no others. The Emperor is grim faced at court although very gentle to his Empress and for now she keeps to her rooms, where he has sent every kind of gift to ease her sorrow: from winter berry branches artfully arranged to platters of sweets and poems in his own hand. This child should have been their heir, all of us know that it would have been his name kept in the golden box behind the throne. After the Emperor's death it would have been opened to reveal the name of his successor, the little boy who has now been taken away. Now the box is empty, awaiting another name. The court waits to see what battle-lines will be drawn. Will the Empress rally herself to bear more children, even though she is now fully thirty-six years old? Or will a younger concubine provide the future Emperor and in so doing supersede the current Empress to become, one day, that most important of all the women at court: a Dowager Empress?

The Emperor is not about to give up hope of an heir from his beloved Empress. When the astrologers tell him that the Empress must not remain in the palace, for fear of evil influences in her chart, he orders that a tour be arranged to Shandong in the south-east. This, he has determined, will be of benefit to her wellbeing. She surely cannot

The Consorts

fail to be stirred by such sights as Mount Tai and the birthplace of Confucius himself. The tour is organised with all due speed and before the first month of spring can reach us a party of courtiers, concubines and our accompanying servants have been selected. I am surprised to find myself and Ying amongst the party, but pleased not to have be left behind as some of the older ladies have been.

"You are to provide gaiety and entertainment," the Chief Eunuch lectures us. "His Majesty wishes for Empress Fuca to be surrounded by happy faces."

I can't imagine that a woman who has just lost her child much wishes to be surrounded by the cheerful countenances of younger concubines, each plotting for their own ascent, but if that's what the Emperor wants, it is what he will get. Servants rush back and forth packing fur-lined robes and thick boots as well as lighter clothes should spring come early. Guards and officials ready themselves and soon thousands of people flood out through the gates of the Forbidden City, leaving it quiet behind us.

The tour is pleasant enough and seems to improve the Empress' wellbeing as planned. She prays at the temple of Mount Tai and the Emperor spends much of his time by her side, their heads tenderly together, her every wish granted. As we move from place to place we accustom ourselves to the new lodgings in which we are placed each time. Ying and I are often placed in nearby houses and enjoy visiting new gardens. Uncalled for, as usual, we spend our time together.

One garden we visit draws most of the ladies, for its large pond and fountains create an attraction. We gather the first flowers of spring and enjoy the warm rays of the sun. I lean over the edge of the pond feeding the eager fish while Ying sits beside me. Most of the other ladies sit nearby, playing board games or chattering amongst themselves.

"When we return to Beijing we will have moved back to the Summer Palace and can go boating again," says Ying and I nod eagerly.

"Always together, always planning to be alone?"

The two of us sit silent, not looking up at Ula Nara's too-loud voice but down at the darting orange fish. Slowly I raise my head and see the eyes of all the other ladies on us. My heart sinks at the unwanted attention.

"You are welcome to join us, Lady Ula Nara," says Ying boldly. I feel a shiver of fear. Ula Nara cannot be so easily got rid of, she can use anything you say against you. It would be better to stay silent but I do not know how to signal this to Ying.

Ula Nara's smile broadens, as though Ying has given her an unexpected opportunity. "I wouldn't dream of it," she says. "Two is so romantic. Three – well that is just clumsy, don't you think?"

Ying's face is growing thunderous. I frown at her to keep quiet but she ignores me and rises to her feet. Ula Nara, even in her highest shoes, is shorter than her. "Is there an accusation you wish to make, Lady Ula Nara?"

The women around us have been quiet, watching while seeming not to watch too closely. Now the silence is absolute and no-one feigns indifference.

Ula Nara's smile doesn't fade. "Accusation? Is there an accusation to be made?" she asks. "I had not meant anything by my remarks but if there is something you would like to tell me, Lady Ying…"

Ying's mouth opens but I grab at her hand and she closes it again, stands silent, her eyes narrow and angry.

"Holding hands," says Ula Nara, still smiling. "How sweet."

I let go of Ying's hand and watch as Ula Nara moves away, still smiling. The other ladies pretend to look away and begin to whisper amongst themselves, still darting glances our way. Only Lady Ling is silent, gazing at Ying and me with an expression of curiosity and interest, head tilted to one side. When she sees me watching her she smiles, not unpleasantly, and holds my gaze too long before I drop my head and return to my rooms, Ying stubbornly remaining where she is. Bao tuts when I relate the story and mutters unpleasant things under his breath about Ula Nara and her devious ways. "Pay no attention to her," he says as he tucks me into my bed. "She will forget about you soon enough and bother someone else."

In the early morning I am still only half-dressed when Bao hurries into my bedchamber. "Lady Ula Nara is here," he hisses.

I can think of no reason why she would call on me at this hour and my belly knots at the thought of yesterday, of her words aimed like poisonous arrows at Ying and I.

"She says she wants to see you."

"Like this?" I say, indicating my loose hair, my bare feet.

Bao gestures helplessly. "She insisted," he tells me and I know that even Bao, for all his loyalty to me and commanding ways in my household, for all his muttered words about her, is afraid of Ula Nara.

I make my way to the living room, where I find Ula Nara standing by the window looking out into my garden.

"My lady," I say, bowing. "You find me unready for visitors."

She turns to look at me, her eyes taking in every part of me from my ruffled hair down to my feet, now encased in little silk shoes to at least keep me warm. She towers over me, wearing cloud-climbing shoes far higher than those of most of the ladies. Her lips curve into something approaching a smirk. "Were you… *busy*, Lady Qing?" she asks.

"I was asleep," I say, "and not expecting visitors." I want my voice to sound cool but I hear my words tremble.

"I came to give you a gift," she says.

I wait, silent. I will not give her the satisfaction of showing curiosity.

She gestures towards a silk-wrapped parcel on my table.

I don't move towards it. Whatever game she is playing, I want no part of it. There is no gift Ula Nara could give me that I would want to receive, of this I'm sure.

"A gift for you," she says. "Something to peruse in your bedchamber, perhaps? Or with … a *friend?*"

I stay silent.

"Well, I will be going," she says.

I bow and gesture to Bao that he should show her out. Left alone, I pick up the parcel and slowly unwrap it.

It is an album of paintings. I have seen such albums before. I was shown them before I joined the court, as part of my education as a future bride for the Emperor and I saw them once in the Emperor's rooms. In such an album there are many depictions of what goes on between a man and a woman. They can be used for private titillation, for the education of young women and men, for lovers to look at together and be aroused. I bite my lip. Why would Ula Nara give me this? I turn to the first page. It is a painting of two women, standing by a tree in full blossom. The robes of the first woman are loose, the second cups her breast in one hand. I feel my cheeks grow warm and turn to the next painting. Two women kiss, their arms wrapped around one another while ripe fruits hang above their heads. I turn each painting faster and faster. Women embrace, kiss, touch one another. They lie in bedchambers among crumpled sheets, undress in gardens, reach out for one another in flower-filled pavilions. They throw back their heads in pleasure and laugh intimately together, their naked bodies entwined.

There are hardly any men. Every album I have ever seen depicts men and women together. Sometimes there are women pleasuring one another, but mostly under the gaze of a man. Here there are almost entirely women, in painting after painting. I stand, holding the album, my eyes unseeing as I gaze at the garden outside. Ula Nara means to imply things about Ying and me with this gift, she means to taunt, to threaten, to make me afraid that she will reveal something about me, about Ying and me, to others. She seeks to find the weak point of every woman here at court and press so hard upon it that those women crack under the pressure, withdraw from any competition for the Emperor's gaze. She makes each woman afraid, uncertain, ashamed that her secrets will be found out, however foolish and unimportant they may be.

I try to comfort myself. I *have* no secrets, I think. Ying is my friend. There is nothing of this forbidden intimacy between us, as Ula Nara implies. The gift is meaningless. Why does she want to target us anyway? I have no interest in the Emperor and have been shown no favour. Ying may be new here but already she has been found wanting. Ula Nara's threat, masquerading as a gift, is without strength, without power. A tiny voice inside me says that this is not true, but I push it away. I am afraid of Ula Nara finding anything in me that she can use against me.

But I find myself hiding the album away. I slip it inside my own personal travelling box of belongings, where my servants will not find it. Even as I hide it I wonder why I do not just hand it to Bao to be disposed of, but I have no answer, even for myself. I do not mention the album to Ying but I am conscious that in the presence of the other ladies now I am stiff and silent with her and I do not allow so much as our robes to brush one another. The days pass and I feel a sad ache for something easy between us that has been lost.

We are reaching the end of our tour and there is a grand banquet, a tedious affair as usual, for there is nothing to do but wear even more elaborate clothes, eat ever greater amounts of food and be admired by the officials and courtiers, whilst speaking mostly only amongst ourselves. Almost everyone is in place, mostly chattering about an unexpected snow flurry, too late in spring to be usual, that chased us all indoors yesterday, but there is a notable absence.

"The Empress has caught a chill and will not be attending the banquet," explains the serving eunuch closest to me, when I raise a questioning eyebrow.

We nod, uninterested. Few of us are close friends with the Empress, for she is always by the Emperor's side. Only Ula Nara brightens and avails herself of the space closest to the Emperor, as she is the highest-ranking amongst us. Ling watches her with a small smile. Ula Nara may be higher-ranked, she can edge her way closer to the Emperor at any banquet or public event she chooses to, but it is Ling who is called again and again to the Emperor's rooms, seemingly without even trying.

The banquet is long and slow. Seated amongst the women there is little conversation, for too many women here think of nothing but how to make their way into the Emperor's affections and do not want to make friends with a possible rival.

In the morning we are informed that the Empress' chill has not improved, so there are few plans for the day and we are left to make our own choices, a rare occurrence on this journey. I wrap up in furs and walk in the gardens, nod to a few of the other ladies. We are bored, we thought we would be heading home by now, but we cannot leave if the Empress is still unwell. I see Ying in the distance and rather than hurry to her side I find myself edging away, wondering whether I can return to my own rooms without her noticing. I am afraid of the other ladies' too-bold stares when I am with Ying, their curious looks and sometimes the whispers between them, as though we were some sort of object of curiosity, some rare breed rather than two among the many women here. But Ying is too quick and she catches me up as I reach my rooms.

"You have to tell me what Ula Nara has done to you," she says, exasperated and out of breath. "You're silent when we are in company and you move away from me any time I come near you. Did she see you again after that time by the fish pond?"

I don't need to ask who 'she' is. I nod unwillingly.

"Well?"

"She gave me a gift," I say.

"Gift? Ula Nara? Why?"

I shake my head at her, for there are maids present. I go to my room and fetch the album of paintings, then lead Ying out into the gardens with me. I hand it to her at arm's length and watch her face as she looks through it. She blushes when she sees what it is but as she leafs through the pages I see her face grow still and her lips part. I wonder if I have shocked her very greatly, if perhaps they do not have such albums in Mongolia. I am about to ask for it back, to say that it is stupid and I will have it thrown away, when I hear footsteps nearby. Too late I see a figure approaching and see Ula Nara approaching. I grab at Ying and all but drag her inside the shelter of a huge willow tree that falls, cavern-like, over a secluded part of the garden. "Shush," I hiss. "Shush!"

We stand pressed closed together, arms about one another trying to make ourselves smaller, listening for Ula Nara's footsteps. She does not call out to find me, nor summon a servant. Instead her steps are slow and cautious, soft as she can make them. I try not to move. I cannot see Ying's face but I can feel her warmth slowly seeping into me through our robes, feel her breath on my neck. She does not hold me stiffly but rather embraces me as though it were the most natural thing in the world, allowing her head to rest on my shoulder, her body soft against me rather than stiff with fear as I am. I take a deep breath to try and calm myself and find myself inhaling her perfume, a delicate thing of light flowers and fresh air after the rain. For a brief moment I forget about Ula Nara and simply enjoy the sensation of being embraced. Bao often clasps my hands and sometimes rubs my back if it aches but I don't believe I have been embraced since I entered the Forbidden City, since I left my family behind, never to see them again. The Emperor perhaps embraced me on those three occasions when I was in his rooms but I was too awkward and afraid to relax into his arms. I have been here seven years without feeling love from another person and now I am embraced. I think for a moment of the paintings, of two women standing beneath a fruiting tree, embracing as we are, their arms about one another, their lips upon one another's lips and I feel a heat rise up in me. I begin to pull away.

But the footsteps have stopped. There is complete silence, broken only by a bird, singing. A brief trill and then silence again. I try to see but all I have sight of is leaves and the grass beneath our feet. Then I see two feet. Perched on blue silken cloud-climbing shoes, their owner shifting from one to the other as she turns about. It is Ula Nara and she is so close she must be able to hear our breathing. In a moment she will see us, for if she looks down she will surely see our feet.

"My Lady Ula Nara!"

It is Bao's voice, his tone surprised, his voice very loud. I see the blue shoes turn away from us towards him and then see Bao's face near the shoes as he falls to his knees before Ula Nara. "My Lady! We have been remiss in welcoming you. Are you lost in the gardens? Are you here to visit my Lady Qing?"

"No – no," I hear Ula Nara reply, her tone reluctant. "I was only wandering. I was – lost, as you say," she adds.

"Let me accompany you back to your own palace," says Bao, all concern. He raises his face from the ground and as he does so catches my eye for a moment. His face does not change at the sight of Ying and I embracing. He rises, and I see him accompany Ula Nara out of the garden, their footsteps fading.

I release Ying. "She was about to find us!" I say. I laugh a little, embarrassed at how long we have been embracing. "If she'd seen us she would have thought all her silly comments were true!" I add, my voice a little too loud.

Ying doesn't laugh. Her eyes are serious as she meets mine. Her gaze flickers for a moment to my lips and then she smiles and looks away, shrugging a little. "Ula Nara sees what she wants to see," she says.

I walk behind Ying as she makes her way back to my palace. Outside it she stops and turns to me. "I will return to my rooms for now," she says, her voice quieter than usual. "I am a little tired."

I nod and smile, then wave to her as she makes her way out of my garden to where her bearers await. Only as I turn back to my own rooms do I think that, in all the time I have known her, I have never heard Ying say she is tired.

We do not speak of Ula Nara again, nor of the album, which I return to its hiding place. But it is as though a heavy burden has been lifted, and we no longer act oddly amongst the other ladies, instead we spend time together as usual, as though daring Ula Nara to comment, but she does not. She has other concerns.

The Empress has grown gravely ill. Her chill may have been of little concern at first but she seems to have had no strength to fight it and now one physician after another visits her rooms and the Emperor is seen pacing the floor. Banquets and other events are cancelled and we are told to pray for Her Majesty's good health, which we do, somewhat bemused by the sudden change in our party's nature – we have gone from pleasure-seeking diversions to carers for an invalid in a matter of days.

At last the Emperor orders that we should embark onto the imperial barges to take us back to Beijing. He is dissatisfied with the Empress' care and decrees that we must return to her own palace, where she will feel more content and recover quickly. Servants hurry to prepare everything and we make our way into the small cabins that will carry us back toward Beijing. Ahead of us is the barge carrying the Empress, swaddled in silken covers and surrounded by concerned physicians.

Night falls and still we have not set sail. Ying is in her own cabin and I feel as though I cannot breathe in my own. I wish she was at my side so that I could talk to someone but we have been told to remain within our own quarters. Lanterns begin to glow along the edge of the canal and looking out from the barge windows I see swaying, shadowy forms lining the banks and hear distant chanting. The air seems full of foreboding.

"Officials and monks, praying for Her Majesty," Bao tells me as he undresses me for bed, shooing away too-curious maids. "Stop peeping out, you silly girls. How unseemly," he tuts.

He doesn't stop me though and I watch as the kneeling shadows bow and bow again. "Is she very ill, Bao?" I ask. The chanting is beginning to grate on me, I want to stuff my ears with something to escape its endless repetition.

"Who can tell," he says, wrapping a sleeping robe about me. "She has been well enough until now. And it was only a chill, she should have recovered by now. But the loss of a child…" He sighs and shakes his head. "Now into bed," he adds, all but pulling me towards the heavy blankets he has arranged for me on my already-heaped up bed. "I will not have you catching a chill as well."

I lie awake for a while. This has been a strange journey for me. I have seen more of Ula Nara than I care to and she has frightened me, for to have her follow you like a dog scenting its quarry is a fearsome thing. I worry for Ying and I, that we will be somehow tainted by her suspicions, and yet I cannot stay away from Ying. She is my friend, my companion, the person who has made my life here more pleasant than it has been in the past seven years when I was alone and forgotten. I am too weary to strategise. Instead I fall asleep and dream strange dreams, of dark shadows that may or may not be Ula Nara watching me, of lips too close to mine which are not the Emperor's but those of an unseen woman.

In the darkness of my bedchamber the barge rocks unsteadily and a hammering at the outer doors wakes me. My household stirs. I sit up in bed, straining to hear. Bao loudly demands to know what is the meaning of this disturbance at such an hour and receives a muttered reply, which leaves him without words. I wait, as the eunuch on guard lights a lantern. I pull a cover about my shoulders, hearing Bao's quick footsteps. The door opens and he stands framed in the shadows.

"What is wrong?" I ask.

"The Empress is dead," pants Bao and with those four words our whole world changes.

Emperor

WE DRESS IN WHITE AND our hair hangs loose down our backs, flowers and gemstones forgotten, a sign of respect and mourning for the Empress. The men's queues are cut short. We look like ghosts wandering about the court, hungry for news, for gossip, for direction now that our hierarchy has been smashed, its glittering shards dangers on which the unwary may tread.

The Emperor is red-eyed with grief. I have never seen him like this. He refuses to carry out his usual tasks of administration, leaving important papers, official appeals and the generals of his vast army without response or direction. The only rituals he will carry out are those involving prayers. He stumbles his way from temple to temple, bowing and praying, praying and bowing, white-faced, his every move surrounded by clouds of incense and chanting monks. He commanded that his Empress' body should be brought back to Beijing without leaving the imperial barge. Sailing up the canal was accomplished readily enough but once close to Beijing the entire barge had to be dragged out of the water on a hastily-constructed wooden track greased with vegetable leaves. Hundreds upon hundreds of labourers were needed to pull the barge through the streets of Beijing to the Forbidden City. The Palace of Eternal Spring, once her own magnificent home, now acts as a mausoleum for her to lie in state, before she is interred. Each of us must visit to pay our respects and more often than not the Emperor is by her side, tears flowing down his face. When my turn comes I don't know where to look or what to say, so I perform the most formal of kowtows both to him and to the Empress' body, my forehead knocking on the cold hard floor, my face hidden from view. When I rise I hesitate, wondering whether I should offer words of comfort or reach out to touch his heaving shoulders. But although I am his concubine, I barely know this man. He might as well be a stranger to me and so I retreat, my footsteps as quiet as I can make them. He does not raise his head.

I see him again in one of the grand receiving halls as he reads out memorials and poems sent by officials and noble houses throughout his empire. They offer tribute to the 'loyal and wise' Empress, praising her beauty, her goodness, her love for the Emperor and his for her. He cannot stop tears falling and has to pause often, but he will not allow his officials to take over the task. I stand silent, amidst the other women of the court, each of us taken aback by the strength of his grief. Even the Chief Eunuch, chosen for his abilities to manage any and every situation, looks lost. How to handle the Son of Heaven when his godlike exterior has shattered like some exquisite porcelain shell and revealed the Emperor to be only a man after all?

There is a pause in the readings and the Emperor sits more upright. He gestures to the Chief Eunuch and there is a consultation, during which his face darkens. We watch, too far away to make out what is being said, all of us women and courtiers straining to make out what is making the Emperor angry.

"It seems," he announces suddenly, his voice stronger, "that certain officials, whom I believed loyal to me, have not seen fit to offer their condolences to me, nor praise our beloved Empress."

"They must be mad," whispers Ying to me. "Why would you not send your condolences? Everyone knows it is the correct thing to do, surely?"

I dip my head in a small nod. Whoever these officials are, if they could see the Emperor's face at this moment they would deeply regret their oversight.

The Emperor stands. He is a tall man. Now he is angry. The court stiffens, no-one daring to move, to draw attention to themselves at this dangerous moment.

"We have been given a list of over fifty names," he says. "Those who have not seen fit to pay homage to our Empress will be punished for their lack of respect. Those from the Han Chinese families will be demoted by two grades."

There's a murmur of sycophantic assent from the court, although nobody cares to meet the Emperor's eyes.

"They have been shown leniency because they are not Manchu," he adds. "They cannot be expected to show the proper behaviour expected of our own people."

Silence. We had all thought that it was the Manchu officials who would be shown leniency. Now courtiers turn their heads to meet one another's eyes, wondering what will happen to those who will receive a harsher punishment. Greater demotions? Exile perhaps?

"These people should have been howling in sadness," declares the Emperor. His voice is growing louder and less controlled, wavering as his eyes fill with tears. The Chief Eunuch looks afraid. The Emperor has never behaved like this before. "They should have rushed forward to beat their breasts in sorrow and make their pain known to us."

The Empress Dowager, sitting close to the Emperor, reaches out a hand and gently touches his, perhaps attempting to calm him, but he takes no notice.

"We have also heard that there are people who have not followed the regulations of mourning. There have been weddings and music within the prohibited period. There have been men who have not shaved their queues and women who have dressed their hair with adornments. There are those who have not worn mourning clothes."

The Consorts

I glance at Ying and both of us shake our heads slightly. There may not have been many of these people but they have been fools. They are about to be punished for something they could so easily have avoided.

"It is intolerable!"

We jump. The Emperor has shouted – no, screamed this last. The sound of over two hundred people falling to their knees is followed by absolute silence, each of us wishing to be anywhere else but here. None of us can see his face when he speaks again.

"They will forfeit their lives for this affront to the Empress Fuca," says the Emperor, his voice breaking on her name.

The court tiptoes. The Emperor, even though he holds the power of life and death, has until now in his reign been known as a peaceable man. Devoted to his duties as ruler, pleasant and even loving to his women, filial to his mother and kindly towards his young children. Now he has shown another side to his character and it is one that none of us wishes to see again. Mourning efforts are redoubled. Ever more tributes are made to the Empress. The courtiers spend as little time at court as they can manage, fearful of making some error, some blunder that will unwittingly earn the Emperor's wrath. The great halls are silent and only the monks in the temples can feel safe, endlessly chanting for the Empress while the Emperor kneels among them.

The bamboo name chips denoting each concubine go untouched on their silver tray in the Emperor's bedchamber. None of the women is called to his side. The days and weeks wear on and still no lady is named as a companion. The women who used to be called on occasionally are lost. They worry, they fret. They glance sideways at Ying and me, at the older concubines, those of us who were never called upon and are afraid they will be forgotten too.

But two women among us have spotted their chance. Even amidst mourning and fear, the court cannot help but speculate on the path that each will now choose. There are only two names on the lips of the gossips. Ling. And Ula Nara.

Ula Nara shows her hand first. She is Manchu by birth, even if her family is nowhere near as exalted as the late Empress'. An Empress should be Manchu and Ling, however much a favourite, is Han Chinese by birth, even if her family have been made honorary Manchus. Does this give Ula Nara an advantage? Could she become the next Empress? Or will Ling be preferred and her Chinese origins be brushed aside? Ula Nara knows that if she wishes to be seated at the side of the Dragon Throne, she has to move – and move quickly. This may be her only chance.

She is seen to offer herself up for the rituals that must be performed. Empress or no Empress, there are tasks that must be undertaken. Prayers at certain temples on certain days. Rituals must be continuously carried out to ensure good crops, good weather, strong children, a powerful empire, a strong dynasty. Some of these tasks fall to the Emperor. Others traditionally fall to the Empress. In the absence of a living Empress, a senior woman of the court must undertake them and now Ula Nara shows that she has not been idle during the many years that she has resided in the Forbidden City. She may have spied on every other woman at court but she has also been learning court etiquette. The days go by and it becomes plain that there is not one ritual that Ula Nara does not know how to perform. Where one of the other women among us, even one of high rank, might stumble or be uncertain, might need some guidance, Ula Nara never falters. She must have watched the Empress at every event she has ever attended, for Ula Nara knows the correct day and time to perform every ritual. She knows every move and word, the correct offering to each deity, each motion to be made. She makes her way

The Consorts

from one event to another, flawless in her execution. Her bows are immaculate, her prayers clear and well-spoken.

"But he's never cared for her," objects Bao. "And surely the Emperor will make the choice of who is to be his next Empress?"

But for once it seems Bao is wrong, for it becomes known that even against the Emperor's grief-stricken and stubborn refusal to appoint another Empress, a higher authority has made herself known. The Empress Dowager, the only person alive whom the Emperor himself must bow to, has made a decision. She insists that a new Empress must be appointed, that a court without an Empress is no court at all. She has forced this request on the Emperor and he has unwillingly acceded to her authority as his mother. And for some reason it seems she favours Ula Nara. She praises her for her grace and poise, for her knowledge of court etiquette, for her extraordinary ability to produce from memory every possible lineage of the Qing dynasty and every dynasty before them. To recite poems appropriate to the moment, to speak with elegance and confidence on any topic. Ula Nara is a seeker and keeper of secrets. Now her own secret knowledge is revealed and it might just earn her the imperial yellow she so badly craves.

"It can't just be because of her knowledge of etiquette," opines Ying. "Ula Nara knows something about the Dowager Empress. Trust me."

I think of the solemn-faced Dowager Empress and can't imagine what possible secrets she could have. "Like what?" I ask Ying.

Ying shakes her head. "She knows something," she insists. "And if she doesn't know then she has made something up."

I think of Ula Nara standing in the whirling snow, her dark eyes watching Ying and me throwing snowballs and laughing. Her secret smile and insinuating words.

"Well whatever she knows, she's about to get what she wants," I say. "She'll be made Empress, you wait and see."

Ying nods slowly. "Maybe then she'll be happy and stop spying on other people," she says, but she sounds doubtful.

But while Ula Nara has boldly shown her hand and made it clear that nothing but the imperial yellow robes will do for her, that she will not be satisfied until she is seated at the Emperor's side wearing the kingfisher-blue feathered headdress of an Empress, Ling seems to have all but disappeared.

"I thought she was ambitious," I say to Bao.

Bao is pinning up my hair. His hands pause in mid-air. "Lady Ling has chosen a different path," he says.

"What other path is there for a lady at court?" I ask. "There's only one path here and it leads upwards to the Empress if you are popular and down to those poor crazed wretches in the back palaces if you're forgotten about or widowed. Every woman wants to be the Empress or as close as they can get. And how many times in a lifetime does the possibility of becoming Empress open up before us?"

Bao shakes his head. "How many Emperors have been born to an Empress?" he asks me.

I've never really thought about it. "I don't know," I say.

"None," he tells me. "Every Emperor has been born to a concubine."

I think about this.

"And," says Bao, "who is the most important woman at court?"

"The Empress," I say without thinking.

Bao shakes his head. "No, she's not," he says. "The most important woman at court is the Empress Dowager. The Empress must bow to her, even the Emperor must bow to her."

"So?"

"So," says Bao. "I don't believe Lady Ling wants to be the Empress. She has a greater plan. She wants to bear the next Emperor, and become the next Dowager Empress. Look at the Emperor's mother, how well

The Consorts

she is treated: he does everything for her, she has only to utter a desire and it is done. She's not even that old, she might live for years and years and be treated always as the most important woman at court."

I shrug. "Good luck to her," I say, thinking of the imperial children who have already died, those whose names were inscribed with such care in the golden box and are no longer living to claim their place as future heirs. "If Ling wants children she'd better make the Emperor start calling women to his chambers again."

The gossip begins slowly, as the autumn leaves turn from green to blazing colours. It seems that at last a woman was called to the Emperor's rooms, and it was Lady Ling, as any of us might have expected. But the next night another woman is called for and this time it is one of the youngest recruits, a girl named Jasmine, whose delicate body and child-like features marks her out as the newest amongst us. Another night and it seems Jasmine has been found wanting, for now a more senior woman is called in and then another. Women are being called every night to the Emperor's rooms and their servants are kept busy, but the gossip grows ever greater, for it seems that the chosen women are returning to their palaces silent, a little downcast, unwilling to boast of their new-found attention.

"And Lady Ling was called last night," says Bao.

"I heard it was one of the others," I say, puzzled.

Bao shakes his head. "She has been called every night," he says.

"No she hasn't,'" I object. "It was Jasmine and then that other girl, the tall one, and then it was…"

Bao shakes his head at me in the mirror where he is unpinning my hair. He takes away the last golden pins and wipes away my makeup. I look into the mirror, my hair loose, my shoulders bare before Bao wraps my sleeping robe about me. His voice is very low. "It seems Lady Ling is at the Emperor's side every night," he says.

"But…" I begin again.

"Every night," says Bao. "No matter who else is called."

I frown. "Are the other ladies lying?" I ask, fumbling at the truth. "Are they not really being called to his rooms?"

Bao looks at me, his head tilted, in silence. I think about what he is saying and can feel a blush beginning as I remember Ula Nara's gift to me. How, leafing through the pages, I had seen the image of an older woman, her robes loosened to expose her breasts, standing by the side of a man, guiding him inside a young woman who was lying back on a table, her body fully naked.

"You may go now," I tell Bao and he leaves me with no further words.

Alone, I climb into my bed and lie still for a few moments before I reach down the side of the bed to find the album of paintings I hid there when we returned from our journey. In the dim light of the two lanterns left burning in my room I open the album and look through the pages. The flickering light casts shadows onto the images, so that they seem to move. I feel my breath come a little faster at the thought of being discovered with such a book and yet I keep turning the pages, looking at each image longer than I have ever looked at them before. When I have finished I hide the book again and try to sleep but it is a long time before sleep comes to me and when it does it brings dreams of entwined bodies and kissing lips, of gardens where petals fall from fresh flowers and breasts ripen like fruits. I awake in the darkness of the night with one hand pressed to my sex and the other tangled in my long hair, my body drenched in sweat, filled with a desperate unfulfilled desire that grips me in its claws.

Morning comes and I sleep longer than usual after my restless night. I wake to the sounds of the servants hurrying about and assume Ying must have arrived. But when I peep out of my room, wrapped in my sleeping robe, hair still ruffled from my tossing and turning of the night, there is no sign of her. Instead, maids are rushing to carry hot water to my bathroom while Bao, red-faced and sweating, is looking over my very finest clothes and seeming none too pleased with them.

"Is something wrong?" I ask, standing in the doorway, ignored by everyone.

Bao turns to me, flustered. "You are called on."

"What?"

"You have been summoned."

"Summoned where?" I ask, still stupid from lack of sleep.

"To the *Emperor*," says Bao, exasperated. "You are his chosen companion for tonight. And there is *nothing* suitable for you to wear," he adds, almost in tears.

I stand, silent. I can feel myself swaying slightly in shock. "I am to be the Emperor's companion tonight?" I repeat. "In his bedchamber?"

"Yes of course in his bedchamber, where else?" splutters Bao. "Now go and be bathed. I have important things to prepare if you are to be ready in time. And tell them to do something about the dark circles under your eyes," he adds, grabbing another handful of clothes and beginning to sound hysterical. "You look *old*." It is the only unkind thing Bao has ever said to me and it makes me realise that this is real, this is actually happening, it is not some strange dream or practical joke.

Why have I been called on now? How has the Emperor even remembered me after all this time? I had assumed I had been forgotten forever, that I would live out the rest of my life here untouched, uncalled for. I feel my skin turn to gooseflesh and my hands shake. I can barely remember what will be expected of me, only that the few times I was called on I cannot have been found satisfactory, for I was not called on again. And yet now… now I am the chosen companion. Why? What has caused the Emperor to choose my name chip from the many dozens presented to him? Was it a mistake? Is there another lady with characters similar to my own name? Did he believe he was calling for another woman? Will he be disappointed when I arrive?

"Where is Ying?" I ask, wanting to tell her what is happening, wanting her to tell me what to do, not wanting her to know at all and yet needing her near me. I need her to give me strength and courage, to make me laugh rather than be fearful.

"Who cares where Lady Ying is!" cries Bao. "Why would we want her here now? Will you go and be bathed? At once!"

I make my way to the bathtub and while eunuchs and maid fuss about me and the hot water turns my skin pink, I am silent and afraid. I emerge, dripping and worried and still Ying does not appear. She has been warned off, I think, someone has told her that I have been called for and now she is staying away, perhaps unhappy that she has not been called on herself and wondering what I have done to draw the Emperor's attention to me. I find myself wondering whether I *have* done anything to draw attention and yet what could I have done? The Emperor is wrapped so tightly in his grief he barely sees any of us, his eyes look beyond us to his own private vision of Lady Fuca's goodness and beauty. The rest of us are nothing but an annoyance to him in comparison to her exalted memory.

Darkness has fallen when the palanquin comes for me. I am shaking in fear and Bao's own hands tremble even as he tries to encourage me. "You are beautiful," he murmurs. "Do not forget that. The Emperor may have been sad at the loss of his Empress but now he is coming out of his grief. He has cast his mind back and remembered your beauty and grace."

I think Bao is wrong but at least he has fabricated an explanation for my being called. I have none. I hold Bao's hand too tightly and he has to pull away so that the bearers can lift my palanquin and take me

The Consorts

to the Emperor's chambers. I look back at Bao, see him standing in the dark, lit only by lanterns, his hands wringing against one another in his fervent prayer that this is the beginning of a new chance for me, that I may suddenly, incomprehensibly, rise in the Emperor's favour.

I sit in the rocking darkness, the only sound that of the bearers' feet as they run towards my fate. I am not proud and excited, as a concubine ought to be as she is taken towards the Emperor's rooms, dressed and groomed to reach the very heights of her beauty. Instead I feel like a small fearful animal, crouched and cold in my heavy silks, dreading what is to come.

All is brightness. Lanterns are everywhere, in every size and shape. Unknown servants surround me. I am led to an antechamber and undressed without ceremony, their hands skilful and quick. I look surreptitiously at their faces but they are bored. This is a tedious, daily task for them. One women or another, what does it matter. It might matter were I Lady Ling, of course, or some other exalted woman. But I am a nobody. My clothes are gone in moments and I stand waiting to be taken to the Emperor, ready to be found wanting once more. I try to think back to the pillow books I was given as a girl, what sorts of delights I might offer up to the Emperor in an effort to please him, but all that comes to mind is the book Ula Nara gave me. I think of the two women in a bedchamber, one naked in a bath, the other kneeling by her side, one hand caressing the breast of the first, her other hand hidden beneath the depths of the water. I must stop thinking of those images. What use are they to me in what is to come now?

A eunuch stands before me and indicates with a brusque nod that I should follow him. I walk behind him, cold and breathless, eyes down. He stops and bows to someone before him, then leaves the room. I daren't raise my eyes.

"Welcome."

A woman's voice. I look up, startled.

A large bed sits within the alcove of the wall, dark red curtains draped around it, tumbled silk coverlets falling from it. On the bed sits Lady Ling, naked. Her loose hair is long and lustrous, her body firm for her age, pleasing enough to the eye. She is watching me, her face amused at my slowly rising colour.

"I said welcome," she repeats.

I don't know what to say. Why is she here? Where is the Emperor? I stare at her, mute.

She laughs. "You were expecting the Emperor, of course," she says. "Your Majesty," she adds, looking behind me.

I turn quickly and find myself standing in front of the Emperor, also naked. He stands an easy head above me and I fall to the floor.

"Rise, rise," he says.

I stand before him. I don't know what is happening here. I do not know what to do. My head whirls. Does the Emperor intend to have us both – Lady Ling and me? Together? I have never done such a thing, have only seen it in the pillow books, as some strange fantasy. I never expected to have to take part in such an act. What will I do? I want to turn and run.

The Emperor walks past, ignoring me. He joins Lady Ling on the bed, settling himself back as though about to watch a play, one hand lazily caressing her hair. He does not look filled with passion, rather a little tired, perhaps a little curious, but not about to ravish either of us. I look, helpless, to Lady Ling.

She smiles, reaching behind her to stroke the Emperor's thighs, her hand practiced and confident, her face serene. "Lady Qing," she says. "His Majesty wishes for some... variety in his companions, and so he – we – have been exploring the delights of the many ladies of the court these past nights."

The Consorts

This explains it, the silences, the many women sent for, their unwillingness to speak of what happened behind these closed doors.

Lady Ling continues. "There are the more mature women and those who are... new to court. There have been those who are differently shaped in their bodies. And now His Majesty is intrigued to find that there are those who have – different tastes – amongst his ladies."

I look at her. I don't know what she means. Tastes in what, I want to ask, but I'm not sure I want to hear the answer. I am cold and afraid and I wish I was anywhere but here. I feel as though I am being mocked. The lavish room feels tight, as though it is too small for our bodies, for our thoughts, for my fear.

"I have asked for a friend of yours to join us here tonight," says Lady Ling. "I believe you know her well. Perhaps the two of you can enjoy one another's company, while the Emperor and I observe you."

I frown at her. A friend? What does she mean?

Lady Ling's eyes flicker to a shadow that moves in the darkest part of the room. I flinch and then feel my shoulders slump in aghast amazement. The shadow is Ying. Naked as I am, her body tightly held at its full height, her eyes fixed on me as though trying to tell me something I cannot hear. Ying.

I lower my eyes at once. My mouth has gone dry. My heart is pounding so hard that I think it may kill me. What am I to do now? The Emperor and Lady Ling want me to cavort with Ying under their eyes, as though we were pages come to life from a pillow book? They want me to caress her – everywhere, to put my lips to hers, her hands to touch parts of me that – that – I cannot bear it. I feel tears come to my eyes, which fortunately no-one can see, so low is my head bent. This night, this demand of Ling's, it will destroy my only friendship. How can this night happen? After this, how will Ying and I be able to act as though nothing has happened and continue as friends? It is not possible. This night, this very moment now is about to take away the only person who has made my life here more than bearable – has made it happy.

"Your friend is more eager, Qing," comes Ling's voice. I raise my eyes a little and find that while I have stood still, Ying has slowly approached me. Now she is only a hand's breadth away from me. She looks at my face, at the tears glistening in my eyes and her face is sad. I think, she knows this is the end of our friendship too, and at that thought a tear falls.

Ying lifts her hand at once and touches my cheek, stopping the tear and brushing it lightly away with her thumb. She does not lift away her hand, she leaves it there, cupping my face and now I feel her other hand cup my other cheek, so that she holds my face between her hands. Her hands are warm, they do not tremble as mine are doing. Her gaze on me is steady and as each tear falls from my eyes she wipes it away gently, without hurrying. Then she leans forward and kisses me on the lips so lightly that I wonder if she has touched them at all. But my lips sting, they burn as though she had pressed herself against me with urgency. Wondering, I lift a finger to my own mouth and touch my lips, but my touch does not burn like hers.

I find I cannot meet Ying's gaze, I cannot look at Ling to see what she wants of me now, what I should do.

"Well," says Ling's voice, sounding as though she might laugh, "Aren't you going to play with your companion a little, Lady Qing? Offer her at least a caress, an embrace?" Her voice is light, teasing, but I can hear the undertone. I am here by command and I must perform. I raise one shaking hand and place it against the warm skin of Ying's shoulder, without daring to look at what I am doing. I will lose my friend, I think, my only friend, for how can we face each other again after tonight? Gently I draw my hand downwards, stroking the skin of her arm, which has grown goose fleshed. I feel her tremble a little at my touch. Is it worth it, I wonder. Is it worth staying here, satisfying the Emperor and Lady Ling's orders, if I never see her again? If she will not look at me again after this night, nor speak with me? I pause at the thought. If she will not laugh with me, row the boats across the lake with me, push me too far and too fast on the swing, giggle when it is not appropriate, allow her hair to grow rumpled in my lap so that the petals in her headdress fall down across my robes when I rise, then perhaps I would rather run from here and be disgraced, forever set aside.

But Ying's hand is on mine and she lifts it and places my fingers against her breast. My hand stiffens but Ying presses her hand over mine so that I have no choice but to cup her breast in my hand. My fingers might be carved in stone, they are so rigid, so unmoving. My skin is cold all over, but Ying's is warm to the touch, indeed she feels hot, as though she is feverish. I draw back a little so that I can see her eyes and they are bright, shining as though she is truly ill. But her lips are curved in a smile and her movements are soft and relaxed, as though she does not find this moment a torture, rather a pleasure. I feel something inside me unfurl. If she will protect me at this moment then I will protect her from the situation that surrounds us. I cup both her breasts in my hands, that they should not be seen by the Emperor and Ling, I lean into her so that my body covers hers and I rest my head upon her shoulder, my hair falling down her back as though it belonged to her head, not mine.

And Ying sighs. It is a tiny sigh, meant for my ears only. Her whole body relaxes under my touch and she pulls me to her, her warm bare arms wrapped around me, her smile upon my neck and then upon my lips, her own soft hair caressing me as she moves. I find myself thinking that if the Emperor had smiled like this, if he had held me like this, I would have been more graceful in lovemaking; I would have known what to do. I find myself caressing Ying as though it were natural that I should do so and slowly I feel a smile grow on my own lips. Is this what I have waited for, then? Is this what it is to love and be loved? I have waited seven years here to be favoured and thought I had failed and yet it seems I have succeeded without even trying. I think back to my laughter with Ying, our adventures together and the petals falling from her hair and suddenly I know that I have loved her, all of this time. Ying's mouth is sinking below my breasts and I stop her, I cup her face in both my hands and look down at her in astonishment at my own thoughts. She gazes back at me and then buries her face in my belly.

She kneels before me as though I were an empress and before I know what is happening her mouth is on me and I feel my whole body tense with the excess of sensation. It is too much. I cannot bear it. I have gone from not being touched, year after year to this… this… I cannot even name it but every part of my body is shaking both with a tight desire and the fear of giving way to it. I cannot succumb. I must stay upright. I must manage my emotions, these sensations, or I will be overwhelmed by them. Only when I feel her hands on me, when her hands clasp my thighs and her long loose hair sweeps my feet do I hear myself cry out and know that I am lost to this – to her – forever. I find myself kneeling too, grabbing Ying roughly, as though she might suddenly escape me and holding her so tightly she cannot move, can only pant against my mouth, my tongue, my teeth as I try to make every part of her my own, to taste every part of her so that I will never forget this moment, however short it is. In the dark light of the lanterns I hear Ling groan and over Ying's shoulder I see the Emperor enter her, his eyes closed, his body thrusting against Ling, whose smile holds the fierce joy of victory. I close my own eyes, not wishing to see either of them, wanting only to be lost in this moment.

It is over so soon. I do not have time to look into Ying's face again before there is a whispered command from Ling and the eunuchs stand ready. The Emperor, sated and held in Ling's arms, is half asleep. Ying and I are led away in different directions. I want to call after her but I have not yet spoken to her in this place and I don't know what to say to her. I want to ask if she is mine, if this moment is a truth between us or only a lie, a play enacted at the behest of the Emperor's favourite that she was powerless to refuse. In the cold courtyard I am helped into my chair and the bearers lift me just as Ying emerges, led to her own chair. I feel every jolt, every movement of silk against the still-wet parts of my body and want to call out to the men to stop, to take me to Ying, but I know that her own chair is bobbing along in the darkness, back through tiny paths to her own palace where her servants will await her, will wait to hear how it went and she will respond with what? With the silence that has marked each woman that has returned from a night orchestrated by Lady Ling? Will she weep to herself for having been made to do something she hated, or will she have a tiny secret smile on her mouth, the mouth that I cannot stop thinking of? I want to tell the bearers to take me to her palace but I cannot do that. I have to return to my own rooms, where Bao awaits.

"Is all well, my Lady?" he asks. Bao knows that he cannot ask what happened, but he is hoping that I will tell him.

"I am well," I say.

Bao shoos away every other servant and sees to my bedtime ministrations himself. As he undresses me he looks me over with care, as though trying to see what happened while I was away, as though he expects to see markings where I have been touched. In truth I am surprised he can see nothing, for I feel as though every part of my skin is marked by Ying's touch, as though I could look down and see the trails of her fingertips across me like streaks of paint on a silk canvas, pale colours where she caressed me lightly and dark stripes where she clasped me with something approaching rage.

I stand alone in my bedroom, wrapped only in a sleeping robe and gaze with unseeing eyes at my surroundings. Was it a dream, I ask myself? It cannot have been reality. Forgotten for seven years, only to be summoned to the Emperor's bedchamber, ordered to cavort in front of him and his favourite – filled with shame and fear and then to find myself held in a lover's arms, looking into eyes filled with desire… I feel as though I could laugh out loud and yet I am afraid that all of it was nothing, that I misread what I saw in Ying's eyes and that our friendship will now vanish under the weight of this new burden, this unbearable truth. I shiver. Last night was everything I thought I could never have. The price I must pay for it may be too high to bear.

Imperial Concubines

"I SEE YOUR FRIEND YING DOESN'T want to know you now," says Bao crossly. "Still," he adds, meaning to be kind but unable to stop himself being a little smug on my behalf, "It cannot be easy for her to know that you are a favourite with the Emperor now and that she is not."

I sit silently by the window and watch the breeze tug at the falling leaves.

"Girl, hurry up!" exclaims Bao, cuffing a maid on the side of the head as she passes him. "Your mistress' bath must be ready at once or there will be no time to prepare her. And she is in favour now, she must not keep the Emperor waiting!" Even when speaking to the maids Bao cannot keep himself from mentioning my new status, the words tumble eagerly from his mouth every time he opens it.

I am sent for every night. Every morning the summons is sent and with each day that passes Bao grows prouder of me. He spends the day preparing me for my time with the Emperor and I spend the day watching the flowers in my garden and thinking of Ying until I see her.

We never speak. Naked, we walk towards one another as though there were no-one else present. In the dimly lit room we know that Lady Ling uses our embraces to titillate the Emperor until he takes her in his own arms but we might as well be alone. Our caresses grow more tender, our eyes lock together, our kisses are gentle, but we do not speak. I do not know how to say what I want to say and if I did, I would want no-one else to hear it. We used to spend our days together and our nights apart and now all is changed. I barely sleep at night, for I am either entwined in Ying's arms or I lie sleepless in my own bed afterwards, whispering words to her imagined self that I have not the courage to utter when she is close. I sleep fitfully in the daytime, a heavy but broken sleep, desperate for sleep and yet unable to rest. By evening I am pacing my rooms with eagerness, my eyes circled with my own dark desire.

"I know you are called for nightly," whispers Bao, trying to stop my constant movement. "I have had sacrifices made in all the temples so that you will continue to be favoured, but I must also warn you against falling too deeply in love with the Emperor. You know that another lady may be called for one day and I do not want you heartbroken when that moment comes. You must be loving and willing in all ways but do not get too swept away."

I want to laugh. I want to tell Bao that I barely glance at the Emperor, that all I can see are Ying's eyes, her body's lines shifting in the lanterns' flickers, that all I can focus on is the touch of her skin, her hair, her lips. That I cannot even hear Lady Ling cry out from the Emperor's bed because all I hear is Ying's soft breath on my skin. I feel the colour rise in my cheeks and nod at Bao, as though I understand his warning and will take it to heart.

Each night I think that tonight I will whisper to Ying, that I will tell her what is in my heart and hear what she replies. And each night I do not speak, afraid of her silence. I wish she would come to me in the daytimes, as she used to, so that we could speak together and I could know the contents of her heart for sure but she does not and I tell myself that she must be ashamed of our nights, that she must go through with them because she has been ordered to and for no other reason. I look into her eyes and think that she looks at me with love and desire and I open my lips to speak but then dare not and when day comes I look back on the night and think that all I saw was fear and anger at her circumstances. I berate myself for a fool and tell myself that all it would take are a few steps from my palace doors to hers, a question, a glance even but I am not brave enough and as the days pass and Ying never comes to me, my night-time bravery fails me. I sit on my porch, rub Fish's long furry ears and hope for a glimpse of her, but she never appears.

And then comes a different morning. The servants prepare for the evening, confident that I will be called for as companion and yet no eunuchs arrive.

"They're late," huffs Bao, still chivvying the maids to prepare my clothes for later on, but time passes and still there is no summons. I catch Bao looking out of the windows and then standing on the walkway and still I am not named.

"Well," says Bao at last, "it seems clear you are not to be called on for tonight. There will be some ceremony for which the Emperor must remain chaste, I suppose. We could all do with a rest, Heaven knows," he adds.

But the days come and go and I am no longer called for. I see Bao passing small coins to servants from other households and his face grows anxious when it is known that other ladies have been called to the Emperor's rooms.

"When you were last summoned," he says cautiously to me, "did anything untoward happen? Anything that might have somehow offended His Majesty?"

I kissed Ying's lips until my own stung, I think. I slipped my hand between her legs and… "No," I mutter. "Nothing unusual happened."

Bao shakes his head and mutters things under his breath, whether promises or threats to the gods, I don't know.

"Is there word of Lady Ying?" I ask casually, as though she is of little importance to me.

"Oh now you remember your old friend," sighs Bao. "Now that you are all alone again? She will not think much of your loyalty."

I feel tears rush to my eyes and have to turn away at the heat in my throat. Does Ying think I do not love her? Does she think I held her in my arms and kissed her because I was told to? Does she sit, now, in her palace and weep because I do not visit her? My hair undressed, still in my sleeping robe, I make my way out to the walkway between our palaces and take a few steps before I pause. She has never come to me since that first night, I think. And she used to come every day, it was she who made herself at home with me and now she does not wish to see me. Whatever I feel for her, she does not reciprocate it. I turn back and make my way to my bed. I refuse Bao's horrible medicinal teas and pull the curtains close around me, cry into my pillows and eat nothing for days at a time until the gnawing hunger is too great and then I eat and eat until I am almost sick with food, as though eating will somehow fill the void that Ying has left in my life.

There is a ceremony at one of the great temples. I do not even know or care what it is but I am required to attend, as are all the ladies. Now, I think. I am too much of a coward to seek Ying out in private but at the ceremony I will see her and when I do I will know by her face, by her glance…

I am up and bathed and dressed too early and sit watching the sun move round until I can at last set off in my palanquin to join the other ladies of the court. My throat is dry when I step out of the chair and I stumble gracelessly, saved from the cobbles only by the quick wits of a bearer. I blink in the brightness of the day and look about me. Ula Nara, of course, edging closer to the Emperor. The other ladies of high status, each hoping that she might somehow shine forth in his eyes, although he seems oblivious to us all. Ling, a secret smile on her lips as she observes the unending pushes for power unfolding around us. I choke a little on the clouds of incense and play my part, looking, looking for Ying but I cannot see her.

"Missing your friend?" Lady Ling has come close to me without me noticing.

"Yes," I say, without hesitation or shame. What shame can I have before Ling, who has seen me do things I never knew I was capable of? "Where is she?"

"Ill, apparently," says Ling. "Nothing serious," she adds with a smile, seeing my face grow pale. "Just enough to keep her from this ceremony. Not enough to worry anyone."

She turns to move away but I grab at her arm. Her eyebrows raise. "Lady Qing?"

"Call us back," I whisper frantically.

"Call you? To where?" asks Ling, smiling as if playing a game.

"Call us back to His Majesty's rooms," I say, as quietly as I can. "I need to see her again, Lady Ling. I need to speak with her. I need to…"

"Why don't you visit her?" asks Ling.

"I – I cannot," I say and I can feel the tears forming in my eyes. "I beg you, Lady Ling," I add, using her full title. If we were alone I would kowtow to her. "Call us back."

Ling shakes her head. "I cannot do that for I am not called upon myself," she says.

"You must be," I say desperately, my voice a little louder. "You are His Majesty's favourite!"

Her smile is wide. "Oh yes," she says and her hand strays to her belly, hidden below her silken robes. Her hand caresses her own body and for a brief moment I see her belly outlined beneath her robes, its proud curve. "I am indeed a favourite, Qing, but I am no longer called on as a companion. Perhaps in due course," she adds, her smile confident.

I stumble away from the ceremony, mutter something about a headache to the eunuch in charge, clamber into my palanquin and return to my own palace. My head is full of calculations that make no sense. Lady Ling is with child. She will not be called back to the Emperor's rooms again for many months and even when she is, she may not need Ying and me to entice the Emperor into her arms. I have heard that other ladies have been called to his rooms, he must have regained his interest in the women he has available to him. I wonder briefly whether I could somehow seduce him and make him call for me but I do not want him to call for me without Ying and if he called for both of us and wanted to touch us, to – to – I do not want that. I do not want him to touch either Ying or me. By the time I reach my own rooms I truly have a headache and I retire to bed even though it is barely past midday, sending poor Bao into a frenzy of concern. I wave him away, turn my face to the pillow and weep again.

I'm woken by Bao hovering near me. From the light I guess that I have slept through the afternoon and the night, for it is early morning.

"I don't want any more of your vile concoctions," I mutter, my mouth dry. "Bring me water and tea and then leave me alone. I am not getting up."

"Nonsense," says Bao, and I can hear that he is smiling. I struggle to open my eyes and see him bustling about the room humming.

"What have you to be happy about?"

"We are all happy," says Bao, turning to me with a beaming face. "As will you be when you hear the news."

I don't ask what news. I suppose he has heard about Lady Ling's pregnancy. It's hardly something I wish to celebrate.

The Consorts

"You are to be promoted," says Bao.

"What?" I ask, thinking that I have somehow misheard him.

"You won't be an Honoured Lady for much longer," he says with great satisfaction. "You are to be named Imperial Concubine. There! Aren't you happy now? Will you stop your moping?"

I go through the motions of getting up, being dressed and having my hair done, while wondering why I am being promoted. Is this from the Emperor's hand, or Lady Ling's? Am I being rewarded for getting Lady Ling with child? "Are there others being promoted during the ceremony?" I ask.

Bao nods briskly, his mouth full of jade pins for my hair. When he can speak he tilts his head towards Ying's palace. "Your friend," he says. "Though I see you two are no longer speaking. I suppose she was jealous of your attention from His Majesty. But I don't know why she's being promoted. An Imperial Concubine, same as you."

I grab at Bao's hand. "Make me beautiful," I say.

"I always make you beautiful," says Bao, but my clasp must be a little too tight, my voice a little too desperate, for he nods more gravely. "Never fear," he reassures me. "The Emperor will see you at the height of your beauty and he will call you back to his rooms."

I feel hot in my heavy court robes. The too-many layers of silk weigh me down, turn my movements slow and clumsy. I fan myself but the air feels warm, no matter how much it moves. I am surrounded by eunuchs, waiting in the dark recesses leading into the receiving hall, which is full of courtiers and the other women of the court, as well as the Emperor and his mother. Court matters are being attended to before my promotion is announced and I know that somewhere in the darkness is Ying, also weighed down in her court robes, teetering on her cloud climbing shoes. I look about me but I cannot see her and I wonder if she has fallen ill or will be led in on another occasion.

"Lady Ying!"

Even as her name is called, I feel her pass by me. She had been somewhere behind me and her silken sleeves brush past mine too fast for me to clasp her hand. I can only watch in the shadows as her new status is announced.

"Lady Ying is promoted, she is made Imperial Concubine!"

The usual list of privileges is read out, the additional jewels and silks she will receive from the imperial warehouses, the servants she will be able to command. She is given a new *ruyi* sceptre to hold, white jade carved into the complex swirls of a mushroom, wishing her longevity and joy. Her ceremony complete, she turns and is guided away into the crowd of women, her own face pale as the jade she carries. I keep my eyes fixed on her face, hoping she will glance my way but her gaze is kept low and I am already being pushed forwards by the eunuchs managing the ceremonial matters of the day.

"Lady Qing is promoted, she is made Imperial Concubine!"

Facing the Emperor, I hold out my hands to receive my own *ruyi* and find that I am holding a reddish wood, carved with the same emblem of a mushroom as Ying's. Our sceptres match, one dark and one light, but twins. I glance at the Empress Dowager, who looks tired and bored. The Emperor smiles at me but his brief glance tells me nothing. As I step aside to listen to the privileges being read out for my own household I look towards the women. Standing side by side are Ula Nara and Ling. Ula Nara's face is confused. She looks from me to Ying and her eyes narrow. She can find no official source for our promotions, only the rumours she has no doubt paid good silver to gather. Lady Ling catches her eye and smiles. Her hand drops to her belly and I see the shock in Ula Nara's face as she realises that her greatest rival is with child and not only that, but has somehow used Ying and me to achieve her goals. When Ula Nara's glance turns back to me I feel myself grow cold under her unyielding gaze. Ula

The Consorts

Nara now counts me as her enemy. I had better pray Lady Ling rises further in court so that she can protect me. By my side I feel one of the eunuchs, escorting me back to the folds of the women. I look about me to see if I can get closer to Ying, but the eyes of the court are on the imperial throne, where the Empress Dowager, sitting beside her son, has risen to her feet.

"My son's loyal and wise first Empress has left us bereft at her passing," she announces in a surprisingly carrying voice. "He is, naturally, full of grief at this loss. But a court without an empress is not a proper court and therefore I have chosen a new empress for my son."

The court rustles and murmurs with anticipation. It seems the Emperor's mother has won after all and he will have to accept her choice out of filial duty. I glance towards Ling and Ula Nara but neither face shows me anything.

"Lady Ula Nara will be the successor to the first Empress," announces the Empress Dowager. "Her own ceremony of promotion will be held in due course."

I swallow. Ula Nara has just reached the pinnacle of power for a concubine and in her mind, I am an enemy. As is Ying.

Step Empress

"Step Empress?" I say. "What's a Step Empress?"

"The title the Emperor is going to grant Ula Nara," says Bao, ready with the latest gossip.

"Not just Empress?" I've never heard of a Step Empress.

"No," says Bao, certain of his facts. "He said he would not have the title of Empress given to another lady."

I sigh. "Will that be enough for her?" I ask.

"I doubt it," says Bao. "Nothing is ever enough for Ula Nara."

He's right of course, Bao's sources are always correct. Ula Nara is made Step Empress and although eyebrows are raised at the title nobody dares to comment. Ula Nara behaves as though she has not heard the full title and since she is mostly called Your Majesty now, it doesn't much matter to the rest of us.

"Not the same sense of style as Empress Fuca," sniffs Bao. "You could hardly fit any more gemstones onto her."

It's true. Where Empress Fuca was not given to ostentation, preferring headdresses decorated with fresh flowers or straw woven into delicate shapes and wearing robes in delicate hues of peaches and pinks, Ula Nara is determined that there should be no doubt as to her status. Almost all her robes are now made in imperial yellow, signalling clearly to each of us that she is the only one of us who may wear this colour aside from the Emperor and his mother. She is elite, different to us. She wears formal headdresses on almost every occasion, towering blue birds and pearls trembling above her head, kingfisher-feather hairpins gleaming in the light. Ropes of pearls are draped over her, her fingers glitter with golden nail shields.

"No one can doubt she is the new Empress," I say.

Bao is not won over so easily. "Empress Fuca didn't have to prove she was Empress," he says. "The Emperor loved her."

I shrug. "Maybe he'll come to love Ula Nara," I say. "In due course." I say it more with hope than conviction. Maybe if Ula Nara felt loved she might stop her incessant jealousy, her watching and fault-finding. She might not notice her rivals so much if she were more secure in her position.

Bao shakes his head. "The Emperor dislikes her jealous nature," he says. "He has always liked women who are different, who hold their own in some way. Like Empress Fuca, like Lady Ling. Ula Nara isn't different. She's an Empress of China, chiselled from jade, moulded from clay. Nothing more nor less."

I don't care how much yellow Ula Nara wears. She can flaunt every jewel in the imperial warehouses if it will make her happy, if it will finally stop her spying and sneaking, her looking out for trouble in every possible way, if it can somehow assuage her need to make others unhappy. I wait, anxious, for her to make a move.

"Lady Ula Nara is made Step Empress," calls out the Chief Eunuch and all of us fall to our knees to offer her kowtows. High on her throne, seated to one side of the Emperor while his mother sits on the other side, Ula Nara's huge headdress of blue birds made from kingfisher feathers and gently dangling pearls sits atop her unsmiling face. Only when all proclamations have been made does she motion to the Chief Eunuch, who nods his head at her reminder and turns back to face us.

"Her Gracious Majesty has asked that one of the Imperial

Concubines should be moved from her current palace to one within the grounds of Her Majesty's own residence. This privilege is given to one of Her Majesty's closest companions."

Closest companions, I think, who might they be? Certainly Ula Nara does not have friends amongst the women of the court. But already something inside me is growing heavy and when I see a faint smile on Ula Nara's lips, see where her gaze is falling, I feel a sharp acid rise in my throat.

"Imperial Concubine Ying is granted this privilege," continues the Chief Eunuch and I see Ula Nara's triumphant glance at Ling and Ling's grim face as Ying is brought forward to stand just below Ula Nara's throne, like a prisoner of war on display by a conquering general.

By the time I reach my own palace she is already gone. Golden Peach prowls the rooftop, yowling. The servants must have been packing while I stood motionless for the never-ending tedium of Ula Nara's promotion and the cat refuses to follow her mistress to a new home. I can't help myself. I stand on the walkway, trying to peer inside. I try the door and finding it unlocked I go from room to room, each of them stripped bare. In her bedroom I find one small jade hairpin and sink to my knees, hearing a strange sound echo around the empty palace. I half-wonder what it is until I realise it is me, keening. Watching my tears fall onto the floor I rock back and forth holding the tiny pin, all I have left of her, all I will ever have of her again if Ula Nara has her way.

"She was still your friend?"

Bao has found me. Gentle old Bao, who held me many years ago when I first came here aged just thirteen, little more than a child weeping with homesickness. He promised me then he would make me

The Consorts

a home here and has spent every day since proving himself both loyal and kind to me. He is the only person in whom I can confide.

"She was still my friend," I sob. "Oh Bao, she was more than my friend. She was my love."

Bao is quiet for a time while I sob, although his hand does not stop stroking my back, each gentle stroke a comfort. When my sobs have quietened he turns me to look at him and his eyes are curious.

"We were both called," I stumble. "To – to the rooms. Both of us. Because Lady Ling wanted to – to encourage His Majesty. And – and – " my sobs return. "She is my love," I manage once again "And Ula Nara has taken her from me to hurt Lady Ling, to show her that she has more power, that Ling may promote us but Ula Nara can keep us apart. Oh Bao!"

Bao says nothing. He pulls me to my feet and lets me keep Ying's little pin. He walks with me back to my own rooms, where he removes my heavy court robes and has teas and sweetmeats brought to me. He does not insist on one of the usual dreadful concoctions from the physician but treats me as he might a child, hand-feeding me little cakes and wrapping me in a silken coverlet. He unpins my hair from its tight fastenings and only when darkness comes does he wrap me in a furred robe, lift up a little lantern and gesture to me to follow him. I open my mouth to question him but he shakes his head and I follow him in silence, grasping his hand when he holds it out to me.

In darkness we walk through the tiny streets of the Inner Court, our steps lit by Bao's quivering lantern and by the larger lanterns that mark out each palace. I have never walked these streets except the time Ying ran with me in the snow. I have always been carried. I have never gone out after darkness, I have always been safely installed in my rooms, my servants in attendance. The Inner Court at night seems like an unknown land, a place of shadows and fears. More than once

I startle at a noise or a movement but Bao's warm hand holding mine keeps me from turning back.

We stop outside the gates of Ula Nara's palace. She was moved here only recently, acknowledging her promotion. Her courtyard garden is larger than mine, her palace far bigger. Tall lanterns burn outside her gates and guards are posted nearby. Bao turns away towards a smaller palace nearby and I wonder at his knowing exactly where to find Ying. I open my mouth to ask him but he must hear even my intake of breath, for in the wavering light he shakes his head and gestures to me to be quiet before taking my hand again and moving quietly to a half-open gate.

And I see her. A hunched figure, wrapped in a crumpled sleeping robe that shows how often its owner has turned and turned again in her bed before rising to sit here, in darkness, alone. No servants to comfort and care for her, no guards to protect her. Alone.

Quickly I step forwards, my hands already outstretched towards her when Bao's hand suddenly wrenches my arm back and pulls me into the shadows. Standing behind Ying's hunched shape is the forbidding height of Ula Nara, recognisable even in the flickering light of lanterns. She stands over Ying, looking first one way and then another, as though she stands on guard over her. I hear her speak although I am not close enough to hear what she says and at her voice Ying gets wearily to her feet and follows her indoors, each step an unhappy shuffle.

"What is she doing in Ying's palace?" I hiss at Bao once we are back in the little lane outside Ying's garden.

"She knows that you would seek one another out," says Bao. "She is punishing you for something. What is it?"

"Lady Ling is pregnant," I murmur, leaning against a wall for support, my heart still beating too fast at the brief glimpse of Ying. "Ula Nara hates us for helping her to give the Emperor a child."

The Consorts

In the dark, Bao's voice is serious. "You had better pray Lady Ling has a son," he says. "Or Ula Nara will torment you for the rest of your lives here."

Prince

"Lady Qing is promoted, she is made Consort!"

Once again I stand in full court dress, heavy with silk and flowers. Details are read out of my promotion. In my hands I twist the *ruyi* granted to me to mark the occasion: a dark wood inset with pearls, which take the shape of flowers, something akin to the almond blossom I first saw in Ying's hair. I feel dizzy and am grateful when I have to make way for the second announcement of the day.

"Lady Ying is promoted, she is made Consort!"

I watch as Ying passes me, stiff and awkward as ever in formal court dress. She has never yet learned to be at her ease at court. I doubt she ever will. I want to help her, to step forward by her side and smile encouragingly as she approaches the throne but instead I stand like a statue, my face unsmiling, watching as the Emperor hands her another ceremonial *ruyi*, this one green jade studded with floral-carved gemstones to mark her promotion. Ying's own announcements are made, granting her all that I have been given, with one difference. She is to move palace again. I startle, but a hand brushes my own and I turn to see Ling standing close by me. She smiles as though to comfort me and when the name of the palace is read out I bow my head to her in gratitude, for I know this is her work. Ying is to be moved back to the palace adjoining mine, our walkways inerlinked. Somehow Ling has seen to it, has whispered in the Emperor's ear or that of his senior eunuchs, and now we are to live as close as is possible here. Ling smiles, confident in her wishes being carried out to the letter. Above

The Consorts

us, high on a golden throne by the Emperor's side, Ula Nara's scowl is terrifying to see but the announcements go on and her objection goes unspoken. Ying will move.

Lady Ling bore the Emperor a son. There were fireworks all night long. Ula Nara may have been named Step Empress, she may sit on a golden throne and be laden with gemstones forever but a son has lifted Ling far higher than Ula Nara has yet to accomplish. Ling has but to say the word and all is done as she commands.

I return to my own palace and Bao, all smiles at my new promotion, chatters as he helps to remove my court robes. "Consort," he says, relishing the word. "Not just a concubine anymore. A Consort. I always said you would do well, didn't I? Didn't your poor old Bao always say that?"

I want to smile at him and agree that his loyalty to me has been absolute, that he has never voiced any of the doubts he must have had when I spent my first years here neglected and forgotten. In his mind he has re-told my story and now, to hear him tell it, I was never forgotten, only waiting for my moment to shine, which has surely come to me in the past year. Promoted twice following a brief moment of favour with the Emperor. Who knows, I may rise even further, and if not, well then at least I am now a Consort, lifted above the common throng of concubines. Now I can retire with grace to a quiet corner of the Forbidden City, not abandoned by any means but simply living a quieter life, as befits a lady of my stature and growing age. I try to nod and force something that looks like a smile, but now Bao is worried.

"You are trembling," he says. "What is the matter? Did you catch a chill? I have always said those ceremonies are too long," he adds, dispatching maids in all directions for teas, medicines, blankets and furs. "Any lady of refinement would naturally catch a chill standing about for hours in those draughty receiving halls."

I let him put me to bed early. I let him stoke up the fires to bring the heat of my kang to near-burning levels, I allow him to force vile medicinal drinks down me. Anything so that he will leave me alone.

It is dark and I am alone. The bed is like a firepit and yet I am still trembling, even as sweat trickles between my breasts. I know that Ying and all her household will have returned to the palace next door. I know that she is there now, that she is lying in her own bed, that if I were to step out of my own palace and make my way along the walkway… if I were to be brave…

The cold outside takes my breath away after the bed. But I breathe in the frosty night air as though it will take away all my pain and fear, all the love I have felt and been unable to speak of. I step down onto the walkway with a sudden quick boldness. I will see her. I will go to her palace now. In the dark, dressed only in my sleeping robe, I will demand to see her. I will tell her all that I have felt for her from the very first moment she came here, an angry fettered eagle. I will tell her everything I remember of her. Dripping and enraged climbing out of the lake, laughing above me on the swing. Her head in my lap as petals fell all around us as we laughed. And that night, the night I first saw her in the Emperor's bedchamber. All I feared and all I felt. The aching unbearable loneliness that has filled my every day since we were forced apart. I will tell her everything. And if I am wrong in how she feels, I will not care. I will have said what is true and my heart will be set free.

A shadow moves ahead of me and I stop, expecting a guard, a eunuch on duty. I am about to command them to stand aside when I see the ripple of a silk robe and Ying steps into the light of a lantern. Her arms are wrapped tight around herself as though she is cold, her face looks pale and her eyes look as though she has been crying. For a moment we simply stand and look at one another. She has lost all her boldness, her bravery, her passion. She looks afraid and lonely and somehow smaller than she really is.

I step forward and take her in my arms and as I do I feel her arms close tight about me, her shallow breath turn to sobs. I hold her so tightly she must struggle to breathe. The words I meant to say, the speech I had prepared, have gone. I have forgotten everything except that we are together again. I loosen my hold on her for a moment and she clings to me. I half-laugh. "I will never let you go," I say and I hear from her gulped sob that she was afraid of this. Instead I take her hand and lead her back along the walkway to my own palace. As we enter I see Bao, coming to investigate what the noise is, a small lantern in his hand. I do not stop and as we pass him he holds out the lantern and Ying takes it from him with a tearful smile, which he returns.

I lead Ying to my bedroom and close the door behind us. In the light of the lantern I remove most of Bao's excessive covers from the bed, before turning to Ying, who is watching me. I laugh and hold out my hands. Setting down the lantern, she steps towards me and I lead her to the bed, helping her into it as though I were Bao before I lie beside her. She turns to me and something of the bright flame has returned to her eyes. She lifts a hand and places it against my cheek as she did that first night and I close my eyes and feel tears run down my face. "Oh my love," I whisper to her. "My love."

The days pass so fast that the sun rises and sets in moments. The nights go on forever. Ying's household must be the laziest in the Forbidden City, for she does not stir from my own palace, until at last Bao arranges things to his own satisfaction so that all our servants come under his jurisdiction and our home is always here. Ying's palace sits empty, dusted when Bao can be bothered with sending a maid there and otherwise used only for storage and servants' sleeping quarters.

We spend our days talking, walking in the snowdrifts of our gardens and the courtyards beyond, eating, unable to leave one another's side. We do not venture far from the safety of our own little world. We avoid the great court rituals and stay away from the other women and their planning and plotting, their constant scheming for a greater destiny. We came close enough to the burning flames of ambition to feel our hairs grow singed and feel our flesh grow hot. I cling to the happiness I have found and seek no other greatness. We are happy, and here in this strange world we inhabit, that is a greater destiny than might ever be wished for.

The pale spring sun warms us as we play a board game. Ying's hair is full of my favourite almond blossoms. We are interrupted when an unknown eunuch is ushered into the room, Bao scowling behind him. He addresses me.

"You are commanded to the palace of Lady Ling," he says.

I stand, heart thumping. "For what reason?" I ask.

"Her ladyship wishes to entrust you with a task," he says.

I look at Ying, who has grown pale. Am I to be taken back to the Emperor as a companion for the night? Are we both to be summoned? I had thought, had hoped, we would be left alone at last, safe in our tiny world within a world, away from the eyes of the court. I do not want to be a piece in the high-stake games Ling and Ula Nara play. They frighten me.

I make my way outside. A chair is already waiting for me, the bearers know that a summons from Lady Ling is to be obeyed at once. I look back at Ying as she stands on the walkway, framed by the doorway. She is afraid of what is to come. I try to smile at her but I can feel that my face is shaped into a twisted grimace, not the easy reassurance I was trying to give her. I close the curtain and feel the chair lift.

The Consorts

Lady Ling's palace is sumptuous. An Imperial Noble Consort may have anything she desires and Lady Ling's tastes lean towards cheerful, colourful excess. Her courtyard is filled with early blooming flowers of all possible shades of red and yellow, her rooms are full of colour and decorative objects. Servants bustle about. I am shown into a receiving hall, given tea and sweets and told to wait.

I can feel my feet tapping and try to still them, only for my fingers to begin clenching and unclenching. I try to breathe more deeply, to think of what I can say if she requests my presence in His Majesty's bedchamber again. Can I bargain with her to avoid the task? I have nothing to offer that she wants.

There is a sudden scurry as multiple servants enter the room ahead of Lady Ling. I kneel and kowtow to her. She strides to her chair, a magnificently carved red lacquered wood, seats herself, accepts a bowl of tea and only then looks down at me, her eyes gleaming. I feel my hands shape into fists.

"Sit," she says. "You and I know one another too well to stand on ceremony, Qing."

My throat feels very dry and I try to swallow again. But if I don't speak now Ling will issue some form of order that I daren't refuse. "I must speak, Lady Ling," I say, still on my knees before her. "I ask you not to call me back to the Emperor's rooms. Nor Lady Ying," I add.

Ling's smile is broad, amused. "I have not called you here for that," she says. "But I see you have grown bolder, Qing. You would not have dared make such a request a year ago."

I stay kneeling. "I do not wish to offend," I say. "I seek only a quiet life."

"A life away from the Son of Heaven?"

"A life away from the games women play here," I say.

"The games can be hard," she says. "But there are great rewards to be won."

"I have my reward," I say softly.

Ling nods and is quiet for a moment. "You are lucky, then," she says at last. "Some of us must continue to play before we win the rewards we desire. I have a task for you," she adds.

I swallow.

"The Step Empress is with child," says Ling.

This moment had to come, of course. The Emperor may not greatly care for Ula Nara but she is his Empress now and he has done his duty by her. She is called to his rooms on a regular basis. Lady Ling is afraid of losing her newly established status as imperial favourite and mother to a possible future heir. But she has a plan, I can see it gleaming already in her eyes. Lady Ling is nothing if not a strategian. She should have been a man, she would have made an excellent general.

"The Emperor is most happy with the birth of our son," she says. "Prince Yongyan is strong and growing quickly."

"I wish him all health and happiness," I say automatically.

"Indeed," says Lady Ling. "But it is as well, don't you think, Qing, to have more than one son for the Emperor to love?"

I can see she is thinking of the Empress Fuca, whose beloved sons, so certain to be the heirs to the throne, died, one after another. She does not intend her game to be lost in this way.

"I wish to have more children," she clarifies. "Ula Nara may be Step Empress, but what really matters, as you know, Qing, is children. Sons. Heirs."

I bite my lip. "I wouldn't know, Lady Ling," I say.

She smiles. "Your lack of children may be of advantage to you now," she says. "I need a woman whom I can trust to raise my son so that I can turn my attention back to the Emperor and give him more heirs."

The Consorts

I hesitate. Has she just said what I think she said? I don't dare to hope for such an honour as she seems to be suggesting. "My Lady?"

She makes a small gesture and a eunuch, already instructed, moves forward from the recesses of the room. He is carrying something and at a nod from Lady Ling he makes his way to me and places a heavy, warm bundle in my arms. I can't even look down, so conscious am I of the burden I am being given. Instead I look up at Ling, who smiles, satisfied at my dumbfounded expression.

"You will raise my son, Lady Qing," she says, her voice loud enough for all to hear. "You will give him every care. Who knows, he may be an Emperor one day."

"Yes, Ling," I murmur, not even remembering to use her proper title. "I will raise him as my own."

She nods. "You may go now," she says.

I rise unsteadily on my high shoes, clasping the warm silk to me, scared that I will overbalance with this unexpected weight. How can she bear to let the child out of her sight, I wonder. But Ling is a practical woman. The only thing better than one son is another son. I have no doubt she will ensure the Emperor gives her more than one son. When I look back at her she has already turned away.

When I reach my palace Ying is waiting for me, her face pale. From the windows I see maids and eunuchs peeking out, no doubt against Bao's strict instructions, too curious to mind his threatened punishments. She frowns when I step out of the chair. "What's that?"

I have no words. I walk past her, nearly tripping over Fish, who gambols around my feet, his tail wagging with interest at the new smell he scents in the air. I indicate with a nod of my head that she should follow me. When we enter my bedchamber, Ying just behind me, I motion to the door. She closes it. Cautiously, I settle myself on the bed and draw back the silk wrappings that all but cover the baby's pale face. He is silent, still, his small face motionless, eyes closed. I have a sudden moment of cold terror. Is he dead, I wonder? Have I managed to kill a prince of the imperial bloodline in the short distance we have travelled together from his birth mother's palace to mine?

But the prince stirs. His eyes open once, twice, fluttering with bleary confusion. At last they open fully and he gazes up at me, his dark eyes demanding to know his whereabouts.

Ying is leaning over my shoulder. "Who is it?" she ask, her voice a whisper.

I find my voice at last, although it is hoarse with emotion. "Prince Yongyan," I say. "I am to raise him." I look up at Ying and see that her eyes are filled with tears.

"He is so tiny," she says, reaching out one finger to touch his cheek. She looks at me, sees that my face is still anxious. "Are you happy?"

"I am afraid," I whisper. "How will I know what to do? How will I know if he is too hot or cold, or if he should be fed or… and what if he falls ill," I add miserably. "I am so afraid, Ying."

Ying shakes her head and laughs, although it is half a sob. "You are happy," she tells me. "You are only afraid because you love him already."

I hold the tiny prince closer to me and he lets out an indignant wail at my too-tight embrace. The unusual noise brings Bao to investigate and he stops short at the sight of a baby in my arms and Ying's happy tears.

"The prince?" he asks. Only Bao would know at once who this child is, why I am holding him instead of his mother. "Are you to raise him?"

"Yes," I say, rocking the baby to try and stop him crying. He snuffles and rubs his face against me.

Bao clasps his hands. "You are a family!" he says in a choked whisper. I see his eyes glisten with sudden pride. If we are going to be a family, I think, then Bao is going to spoil this child beyond all measure.

I feel Ying's arm curve around my lower back as she gently sits down beside me.

The baby prince looks up at us – Ying and me, our heads together, faces awestruck, Bao's beaming face hovering above us – and he smiles.

Notes on history and characters

Because this is a novella I have considerably condensed the time period and the events that happened within it. From Consort Qing first entering the Forbidden City to the birth of Prince Yongyan would have been about twenty years. Consorts Qing and Ying were not lovers as far as anyone knows, although erotic paintings of the time often show two women together and men with more than one woman, as depicted in the story. At the time when this novella is set homosexuality had been made a recent offence in China, but it had been quite widely accepted until this time. There are various stories of concubines having affairs together or with their eunuchs.

It was common practice for a concubine not to raise her own child but for it to be given to another concubine. Consorts Qing and Ying each brought up one of Lady Ling's sons. Prince Yongyan (entrusted to Lady Qing), became the next Emperor of China. Both of them were posthumously promoted for their care of the two children, Lady Qing in particular ending up being an Imperial Noble Consort, the highest rank below Empress.

The two women were promoted in the same year from Honoured Ladies to Imperial Concubines and then Consorts, after the death of Qianlong's first Empress. I could not find any obvious reason why they were promoted (there was no coronation, birth of a child, etc.). Neither of them ever had children of their own, implying they

The Consorts

were not great favourites, yet they were given charge of Lady Ling's children, who was herself most definitely a favourite of the Emperor.

Empress Fuca, the first Empress, died suddenly after what seemed to be a minor chill following the death of her son and the Emperor was stricken with grief, reacting very badly to anyone that he did not deem to be mourning properly for her. They had been together since they were teenagers and seemed to have had a genuine and loving relationship. He was very unwilling to appoint another Empress but his mother insisted and forcefully backed Ula Nara.

Ula Nara eventually went mad (rumour had it with jealousy over another woman) and was banished from court. The Emperor refused to appoint another Empress.

Ling was the birth mother of the next Emperor of China (Prince Yongyan), but did not live to enjoy the role of Empress Dowager. She was posthumously made Empress. I have made Prince Yongyan her first son, although she actually had a previous son who died very young.

In 1760, about two years after this story ends, the Emperor conquered a territory to the West (Xinjiang), from which arrived a new, Muslim, concubine. Her legend is told in *The Fragrant Concubine*, a full-length novel in which the Emperor, Ula Nara, Ling, Qing, Ying and little Prince Yongyan appear again.

The names of concubines were regularly changed throughout their lives, usually at each promotion, so tracking one person can be tricky! I have chosen to keep the same names for each concubine regardless of their promotions and the names given are those I used in *The Fragrant Concubine*, so they reflect the names they held as Consorts. These names are actually their family names, not personal names, which were often not set down in the official court records. I have therefore used them as though they were personal names rather than invent names for each woman.

Read on for a preview of...

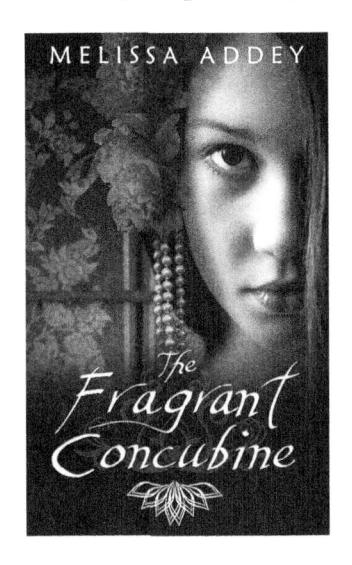

A full-length novel set in the Forbidden City of the 1700s, ***The Fragrant Concubine*** is based on the true story of a Muslim woman sent from a conquered land to be the Emperor's new concubine and the many legends that grew up around her.

The Historical Novel Society's Editor's Choice: *I enjoyed the human drama, the love and hurt, the scheming for revenge, rivalries and loyalties in the Forbidden City. Reading this novel was a moving and wonderful excursion into a different time.*

Before

H E TRAILS MY FOOTSTEPS LIKE *a whipped dog. When I turn to him his eyes flinch away from the cut, the ragged edges now held together with crude stitches, still seeping pus. He looks down, away, over my shoulder, fixes his gaze on the fastenings of my sheepskin jacket.*

But I have just seen something that took my breath away, that numbs both the stinging pain and the crushing defeat of all my plans. Something – someone – that makes my head lift up again.

"Did you see her?"

Nurmat's eyes flicker to my face and then hastily away. "Who?"

"That beggar girl."

He shakes his head, uninterested.

I turn away from him, look about. "She was begging outside the mosque after prayers. We have to find her again."

"Why?"

"So you can see her."

"Why would I want to see her?"

I ignore him, scan the crowd, twist my neck this way and that, oblivious to the passersby who stare at my face. But the girl has gone, slipped away somewhere. I turn back to Nurmat, catch him looking at the cut, his eyes filled with tears he cannot hold back. "We will stay here tonight."

"Why?"

"Find us an inn."

He obeys me without further questioning. He does whatever I ask of him now, since that one moment, the sharp blade's quickness against my skin. His shame is too great to rage against my plans as he used to. This morning, looking in the mirror, my fingers tracing the open wound before it was clumsily sewn back together, I had thought that all was lost, that I must resign myself to a different life. And there was a part of me that was glad. I thought of Nurmat's arms about me, of his mouth upon my lips, and I felt such desire for him, for my new life. But rising from my prayers I heard a plea for alms. When I turned to place a coin in the outstretched palm I looked into her eyes and my heart leapt in recognition. I must see her again, to know if I saw true.

When we rise the late summer morning is cool and the traders have not yet found their voices. We walk through the warren of the city streets until I am dizzy and sick with turning my head this way and that to find her. The market-day crowds began to grow all around us.

Nurmat lays his hand on my arm. "Iparhan," he begins. But I pull away, breaking into a run, pushing my way through the people. I stop so suddenly that Nurmat collides with me and sends me sprawling but I rise at once, ignoring the sting of my grazed palms.

"There!" I say. "There!" Her ragged skinny frame making its way through the crowds. Her face... I wait for her to turn my way and when she does I feel my body begin to shake. Her face is my face. From before the quick blade swept across my cheek. I pull at Nurmat's arm. "There!" I say.

Nurmat turns his head, blinks in confusion as he tries to follow my pointing finger. Then he sees her and grows very still. When he speaks his voice trembles. "No," he says. "No, Iparhan. You said it was over."

I lie to him then. I have never lied to him before. "She will take my place," I say. "I will use her as a spy. Nothing more. If I have information from the City then I – we – can bring about a rebellion. It is a new plan."

Nurmat grips my arm so hard it hurts. But not as much as the hope in his voice. "Swear," he says. "Swear you will not..."

I put my hand on his and I lie again. "I swear," I say. "A spy, nothing more. Bring her to me, Nurmat," I said. "Make sure she has no one: no family or friends to seek her out. Then bring her to me."

He nods and begins to follow her, moving away from me. In that moment I know that our happiness is lost. I could call him back to me, could change my mind and live a gentle loving life by his side.

But it is too late to turn back now.

Market Day

"REMEMBER, MY FRIENDS – ALL legends are true, even the ones that never happened. For in them we find ourselves."

The spit bubble I'm idly blowing bursts unexpectedly. I wipe the spittle off my chin with my sleeve and watch the crowd around the old storyteller disperse; a few small coins tossed his way by the more generous. He always begins and ends with this phrase when telling his far-fetched tales of wild adventure and passionate love, savage monsters and epic journeys. I don't know if he truly believes it or whether he just thinks it adds an air of mystery – after all, all storytellers need an air of mystery about them or they'd just be common beggars with a fanciful imagination. You need to stand out from the crowd here, have something special to make people seek you out. Market day is the day when such storytellers earn their living, and the market of Kashgar, sitting on the trading routes, draws more crowds than most. Being known as a good storyteller here is important.

Now he tucks the coins away and prepares himself for another performance, scratching his balls through his layers of ragged clothing and taking a long drink of water from a dirty old jug, chipped round the edges. He wanders off to find a quiet spot where he can relieve himself before beginning another tale of mystery and romance. His eyes are growing milky but he would know his way round these streets by memory alone. His space is stolen by a troupe of acrobats, flipping this way and that, walking on their hands as though it were the easiest thing imaginable. It isn't. I tried it once when I was a child. I had strong arms even then but I fell over almost immediately and struck my face on an old root. Got a nosebleed for my effort rather than applause.

I start my daily rounds at the mutton dumpling stall of old Mut, tucked down a little corner street on the edge of the market. "Anything for me?"

He shakes his head. He'd give me the split or burnt dumplings but he doesn't care for me enough to give me dumplings that he could sell. "You're too old to still be wandering the streets, girl," he admonishes me. "Find a husband and settle down."

He's been saying this for years. "I don't need a husband, Mut, I manage well enough on my own."

"No one can manage on their own," he says, keeping his eyes on the bobbing dumplings. "Everyone needs a family. People to look out for you."

I shrug and start to turn away when I feel a hand stroke my behind. I smack it away without even looking. "Get your hands off me, you fat good-for-nothing."

Mut's son leers at me through a half-chewed mouthful of meat and bread. "I'll marry you," he says thickly, not bothering to swallow before he speaks.

I make a face. "Spend my life as your slave? No, thank you. Why don't you help your father earn a living instead of sitting about pawing women and stuffing your face?"

Dejected, he goes back to his food as I head towards the main square. I'm almost out of earshot when he calls after me. "Someone was asking about you earlier!"

I ignore him. Maybe someone who caught me stealing food wants to find me and give me a hiding. I'm hardly going to seek them out.

I thread my way back through the crowds and settle down to watch the acrobats.

"Tell your fortune?"

I jump. The voice is right by my ear. I turn and there's an old woman behind me. Her clothes are nothing so much as layers of rags, and there's a thick sweet smell about her which I know is opium, though where she gets enough money for it I don't know; perhaps she uses the cheap stuff mixed with even cheaper tobacco.

I raise my eyebrows. "Slow day?"

She shrugs, her eyes darting about to either side of me, looking at the market-day crowds over my shoulders. "Once they see one person being told their fortune they all come running."

I laugh. "Only if it's a good one, eh?"

She grins, showing a surprisingly good set of teeth still in her head. "Of course."

I grin back. A slow day for her means a bowl of noodles for me. "You'll give me the usual?"

She looks about and lowers her voice. "I've something will make your day brighter?"

I shake my head. "No flowery dreams for me, thank you. Noodles are what I want."

She agrees, grudgingly making it clear it's to be a *small* bowl. If I refuse her offer she'll soon find someone else who will accept.

I settle down on a crumbling wall nearby and present my face for her inspection.

She picks up two wooden rattles and hits them together rhythmically, indicating a fortune-teller at work. The noise attracts people's attention, and two or three bystanders wander over to listen in on my fate.

She runs her hands over my face and looks at me intently. Her voice is louder when she starts to speak, my fortune apparently being of more interest to the complete strangers hanging about than to me.

"A dainty face," she starts. "What a fine face for a poor ragged girl. Her face may bring her great good luck."

I've heard this fortune so many times I roll my eyes. She pinches my ear hard. I'm supposed to look rapt, not disbelieving. I try harder, fixing my eyes devotedly to her face and thinking of hot noodles. This seems to give my face the necessary attentiveness; she pats my cheek and carries on. "Good luck will come from this face," she practically shouts. "A great man will love such a face."

I try not to snort and she grabs my hands, lifting and turning them so the crowd can see. "Such coarse little hands here, so rough. Perhaps your face will bring softness to your hands one day. I see a great man, a man who will let your hands rest only on silk."

I can feel the onlookers getting closer; a few giggles tells me that the old woman's favourite kind of customers, silly young girls with more cash than sense, are edging forward, beginning to hope for their own turn.

"Silk, yes," she goes on. "Dress you in fine silks, he will, and give you jade pins for your hair. Your face will be your fate."

I know she's almost done with me. The real customers are lining up. She likes to keep my fortune short enough to draw them in, not long enough to let them wander away again. I can hear the chink of little coins being turned in impatient hands. My bowl of noodles is getting closer.

"Who amongst you can guess your own futures? What turns of fortune may come your way? Even now the Emperor of China, so far away in Beijing, sends his armies here and claims our lands for his own, from one day to another. Now we are his subjects, his to command. Our people have fallen, our leaders lie silent in their tombs, their heads taken as trophies."

There are some mutterings in the crowd. Quickly she brings their attention back to my shining future rather than their uncertain present. These people are tired of wars. There's been too much fighting in recent years. If the Emperor has taken our lands now, let him have them. Life goes on here on the streets as it always did. Our taxes go to a new master; different officials oversee the trade routes. What difference is there? Wars bring death; taxes bring the same old hardships that can be borne more easily. They want to forget the sorry past and dream of a richer future, so she presses on. "This young girl now, so raggedy and with rough hands, who but I could know she is destined for silks? Are there others who wish to know their fates?"

There are murmurs and little excited pushings amongst the nearest girls. She lets go of me so I stand up, ready to make way for fee-paying customers. She slips me enough for a small bowl of noodles as agreed and I nod, pretending that I am the one paying her. I move past her towards the nearest noodle stall when suddenly she turns and grabs my arm. Behind her sits an eager girl, clutching a coin and lifting up her face, hopeful of another rich generous man appearing in her own future. The fortune-teller ignores her. Her eyes are fixed on me but they seem glazed and her voice is slow. I suppose it's the opium taking effect.

"Where'd you get a perfume like that?" she asks.

I stare at her. "What?"

She leans into me and I pull back a bit for she certainly doesn't smell like perfume. She inhales deeply, her eyes closed. "That. That's…" She thinks for a moment and then shakes her head, almost losing her balance. She clings more tightly to my arm to keep herself upright and opens her eyes. "Don't know what it is, never smelt anything quite like that. Expensive, though. That's the kind merchants bring from a long way off and what rich ladies wear. Not the likes of you. Where's it from?"

I shake my head and pull away. "I'm not wearing perfume. I carry nightsoil, if you like the smell of piss. Where would I get perfume?"

"Some rich man?"

"I'm not that kind of girl."

Her eyes lose their glazed look and now she's focused on me rather than her restless customers. She's never looked at me so steadily or for so long.

I stare back at her. "What?"

She shakes her head, confused. "Don't know. I smelt a perfume on you."

"I told you, I don't wear perfume."

She's frowning. "I know. But I could smell it. It was very strong and then it faded away."

I wink. "Maybe the great man'll give it to me. You know, the one who's going to dress me in silks and have me sitting around doing nothing all day."

I think she'll laugh and let me go, or tell me to keep it down so her customers don't hear me being flippant about her fortunes. She doesn't, though. "Maybe," she says slowly, and turns away.

I puzzle over it for a moment, even sniff my own arm to see if I can smell an expensive perfume. I can't, of course. I smell of a faint stench left over from the dawn when I carried pails of nightsoil to be dumped away from the city walls. The tight-fisted foreman only gave me a thin vegetable broth for my troubles, though, instead of the coin he owed me. I made sure to be clumsy after that so that one of the buckets fell over, leaking a foul mixture of piss and shit all over the doorway of one of his best customers, a fancy house in the centre of town. The broth's all I've had today, so a bowl of noodles is more interesting right now than the opium-raddled ramblings of a so-called fortune-teller.

I order a small bowl and smile nicely at the vendor, hoping he might add a bit more. He doesn't. I take the bowl and squat nearby, scooping noodles into my mouth as quickly as I can. They're gone before I've had time to savour them.

I hand my bowl back to the stallholder and make my way through the crowds. It's slow work to move about on market day. The warren of narrow city streets, squeezed in by high sand-coloured buildings and lined with stalls, swarms with people. I'm surrounded by the bleating of sheep, bellowing of camels, the slow wooden wheels of carts and above all the chattering of people. Cages of live hens and partridges are everywhere, cackling and shrieking as they're lifted out by their feet. The women gossip their way from stall to stall making a simple purchase of dried fruit or nuts last hours. Meanwhile their menfolk are no doubt claiming to be equally busy buying stock – sheep or camels, perhaps even a horse. This, too, seems to take up a great deal of the day. There are acquaintances to nod at, relatives to embrace, wrestling to watch or even take part in, perhaps a spiced lamb pie to eat, bartering being hungry work even if you don't do much of it.

Here and there the Emperor's officials make their way about, consulting records that show them the names of merchants who owe them taxes. They have guards with them in case there's any reluctance to pay up. We're used to the sight of soldiers by now. Young men who fancied themselves rebels used to attack them in the narrow streets after dark – and paid with their lives. Most people kept their heads down and avoided trouble. But now the fighting is over. The Emperor has won and if all he wants is glory and taxes, then so be it. A little boy sticks out his tongue at the soldiers as they pass by but they don't notice him. They wouldn't care if they did. They don't expect us to love them.

I wriggle past two gossips and find myself close to a dried fruit stall where a rich lady is buying whole handfuls of dried raisins. My mouth waters for their sweetness. The lady is fussing over their quality, looking them over disdainfully as though she might command finer things. But raisins in Kashgar are the very best that money can buy and so she can sniff and look down her nose for only so long before she graciously permits the stallholder to sell them to her. Now she turns away, her servants bobbing alongside her carrying many baskets and bundles. She has been busy spending her money today. As they pass me I follow behind the most stupid-looking servant, the one who is carrying foods rather than being entrusted with the more delicate pottery or silks. One quick pull and a handful of raisins is mine. The motion makes the basket rock, though, and a twist of spices falls to the ground. I've already slipped away from them and found a low wall to crouch behind, the raisins hidden inside my too-big man's jacket, so I can watch the lady's fury as others might watch a play.

"Fool!' she shrieks.

Someone ought to tell her she sounds like a common peasant woman instead of the gracious lady she likes to imagine herself. The servant ducks, expecting the slaps coming his way. The first blow catches his shoulder instead of his head, which doesn't satisfy his mistress, so she goes for him again and this time, perhaps realising it is better to get it over with quickly, he doesn't move much and the blow of her hand knocks off his little cap. "Useless, good-for-nothing! The very next market I shall buy a new servant, for you're not worth the sorry few coins I paid for you!"

I grin and settle down in the dusty street behind the wall, cramming sweet raisins into my mouth till every last one is gone, even the ones that fell in the dust when they slipped through my fingers. A little scruffy white cat with a shrivelled leg rubs against me and I stroke it till it purrs and settles down to sleep on my legs, a small embrace from a living creature, a warmth I am unused to. For now my belly feels at least partly full and I sleep for a while in the afternoon sun, hidden from passersby.

It's early evening when I'm woken by drunken singing nearby. I hurry to the nearby mosque, anxious not to miss evening prayers. I pray at the back of the women's room and loiter about afterwards. Sometimes praying gets you a coin from a wealthy woman, it makes them feel pious to give alms to a poor street girl. I've never been taught to pray properly but I can join in with everyone else, go through the motions and murmur scraps of the right words. The bright tiles decorating the mosque are cold to kneel on without a prayer mat but I make do. When winter comes the mosque's a brief respite from the wind. But today no one feels generous and when prayers are over I move off through the crowds, which are now less focused on bargaining for household goods and are happily settling down to the real business of the day: entertainment. I can hear old tunes being sung, gasps at the acrobats who have moved on from their warm-up of walking on their hands and are showing off finer skills with juggling and injury-defying leaps and twirls in mid-air, using all manner of poles and ropes to thrill the crowd. In nearby inns there are drinking games being played, which start off with a literary bent involving reciting poems but become decidedly bawdy as the night wears on. Men sit in the street with their heads tilted back, being shaved or massaged, their tall felt hats on the ground beside them. They munch on almonds and figs, risking their throats being cut when they swallow too close to the strokes of the sharp blades.

I wander away, down other streets. There's one more place to visit before the day is over.

"So, can a pretty girl show me the many delights of Kashgar, eh?"

My grumbling belly has brought me to a small lane with a tall pole at one end, embedded in a yellow earthen wall. It's one of the women's lanes, a place where they wear more ribbons and silks than you'd think would fit on one body and where local men and merchants from further afield come to see what pleasures their money will buy.

When I was a little girl I used to come and stare at them, till I found the customers began to stare at me too closely for my liking. These days I have to be careful round here, but sometimes it's a risk worth taking.

The man is fat and balding, and very drunk. He's barely standing straight. He has his cock in one hand, supposedly ready for action, though it looks a bit limp to me. If he were less drunk he'd see I'm not even dressed like a serving maid to one of the pleasure-women, let alone being one of them myself, but he's a merchant and this is what he is looking for. Merchants come here from all over and it is said that in Beijing they sing rude songs about the girls of Kashgar and their supposed charms. He's just right for me, though, too slow and drunk to grab hold of me. I push him away and he sways dangerously, grasps the pole to keep his balance and fumbles in his robes.

"Got cash," he burbles. "Got strings of it." Sure enough he pulls out a string of coins with his free hand. "How much, then?" he says, because even in his drunken state he can see I'm not running off, that all my attention is fixed on the many swaying coins threaded together on a red string.

I look at the dangling string of cash. Usually they hold up a single coin and I can sometimes grab it and run. I'm too quick for them to chase. But a whole string of coins… I could eat meat instead of noodles every day till next market day.

"Well?" says the man, and then he falls over and lies there at the foot of the yellow wall.

I'm scared he's died for a moment, but then he starts snoring. Much to my disappointment he's fallen on top of the string of cash, so I can't even grab it. I'm a strong girl but he's huge; I'd never roll him over in his state.

I look down the lane. A stout woman I've seen before, who runs one of the brothels, has come out of her doorway and is watching me. "Help you?"

I gesture to the man lying by my feet. "He's got cash and he wants a good time."

"You going to show him it then, are you?'

I shake my head.

She comes a bit closer. "Ah, you again. You keep coming back to look down the lane. Made up your mind to come and work for me?"

I shrug.

"Thinking about it?"

Of course I have been. What other choices do have? Winter will be here soon and how many more winters will I be able to survive alone on the streets? Last year I thought I would die in the cold. By spring I was nothing but bones, my skin stretched too tight across them. The lanes would mean warmth, food. But the price I'd pay for them… I stand silent before her while she waits for the answer I'll have to give one day. I can't bring myself to give it yet. I keep hoping I will think of some other way.

The woman laughs. "Well, some men like a quiet girl." She squints at me and makes her voice softer, coaxing. "I look after my girls. They wear silk, you know. Not all the girls do."

I look down. The fortune-teller's words about my hands resting only on silk come back to me and I wonder if this is what she sees for me each market day. If she really sees anything at all.

"I feed them well too," she says. "Doesn't do to have a scrawny girl about the place."

I look up and she smiles, seeing the first flicker of real interest. "Come and see."

I step back.

"Just a peek," she says.

"I won't stay," I say.

"Of course not," she says. "But a peek won't harm you."

I hesitate, then step forward. She smiles and takes my hand, but I snatch it away.

"All right," she says, laughing at me. "No touching."

We get closer to the house and she points me to a small door. I put my hand on the doorframe for a moment, then step inside.

There is a little courtyard with the house built around it. There's a terrace above us. In the yard are cushions, a table or two and a scrubby little oleaster tree, its fruit slowly turning to gold from grey-green. There are customers here already, half-naked girls sitting on their laps. I step back and bump into the woman who is right behind me.

"Don't worry about them," she says. "Come and see the other girls."

We step away from the courtyard into a room. It's painted in bright colours and there are a few women sitting about on cushions. One is having her hair combed; two are mending clothes. One is smoking a waterpipe, staring into the air.

"My girls," the woman says, waving a hand at them and smiling.

They turn round to look at me.

They're not girls. They look old and tired. The bright silks they wear are cheap and thin, with patches of faded colour where the poor quality dye has dripped away on laundry days. Here and there are stains that haven't washed away so easily. The smell of tobacco is thick in the air.

I turn to face the woman.

"Want to eat with us?" she says, smiling. "There's good food cooking."

I've already smelt the air for food and what I smell is old fat, used again and again. I shake my head and walk towards the door.

She grabs my arm a little too tightly. "Won't you stay?"

I shake my head.

She smiles. It's not the nice smile from before; it's wider and shows her missing teeth. "You'll come back one day," she says. "They all do. You can't last much longer on the streets, a girl your age. A child might receive alms; a young woman might get more than she bargains for. We'll be here when you come back. When the autumn sun's gone and winter gets cold."

I pull away from her and walk out, through the courtyard and back down the lane. I walk slowly, my back very straight because I'm afraid someone will chase me if I run, but my heart beats fast until I find myself in the safety of the market crowds again. The familiar sights – the knife stall with the decorated handles, the delicately balanced piles of eggs, the hat stalls adorned with every colour of velvet and felt shining with bright embroidered threads – surround me and I breathe deeply.

"Thief!"

The man grabs at me but I've already stuffed the hot *naan* into my mouth and made my way down a side street, the bread flapping down over my chin like a giant tongue. The market of Kashgar is no place for a grown man to try to chase a girl who can slip through the crowd at speed. I hear him shout again but it's already a distant sound. I'm safe.

I've found a dark corner between two buildings to crouch in while I eat. Not that there is much left to eat now for I can run and eat at the same time. Hands are better used to make my way in the crowd. My face contorted grotesquely as I made my way down the narrow back streets and now there is barely half a *naan* left. I finish what is left of it in seconds, barely chewing, struggling to swallow great chunks of it. It doesn't do to take your time with food when you might get caught.

I yawn. The earth walls here are hard but the area is growing quieter as the traders finally pack up, grumbling about a poor day's takings. The wind grows a little chill and I pull my hands into my sleeves. I could just stay here for the night I suppose; the earth is still warm from the day's sun and I can't easily be seen by anyone. I stretch out my legs in front of me and yawn again.

"You took some finding."

I leap into the air and come tumbling down, my knees hitting the ground so hard that I cry out. A strong hand slips over my mouth and another pulls me upright and steadies me, for my feet are somehow bound together, though I can't see by what. I try to turn to see my attacker but he doesn't let me move.

"Stand still," he says, his voice low in my ear. "I'll loosen your feet but you're to walk with me as though you were my servant, do you understand?"

I don't reply. There's a hiss before I feel a tiny patch of cold on the nape of my neck. It pricks and I know it's a knife. A sharp one. I nod, downwards only, keeping my head bowed so that my neck no longer touches the knifepoint.

"Good."

The man moves his hand from my mouth to my shoulder, stoops and cuts whatever was tying my feet together. I tense, ready to run.

"Don't," he says. He sounds calm, not angry, which somehow is more frightening. "I found you this time, I'll find you again."

I lift my chin. "Don't count on it."

He tightens his grip. "A man's holding you at knifepoint and you're talking back instead of trembling like a good girl should?"

"I'm not a good girl."

"No," he agrees. He sounds amused. He keeps a hand on my shoulder. I still haven't seen his face. His hand, though, I can see out of the corner of my eye. It's well formed and smooth, not calloused. A young merchant's hand perhaps, not a peasant's. "Now," he says. "I'm not sure I trust you to walk behind me like a servant girl should.

Maybe you ought to pose as my wife instead. That way I could keep a hand on your shoulder as we walk."

I don't reply.

"Awkward one, aren't you," he says. "Never mind, we'll soon cure that."

He keeps one hand on my shoulder and with the other puts away the blade and I feel him twist to grasp at something. He pulls away my ragged jacket in one hard movement.

I gasp. "Don't – don't!"

I struggle under his hand and at once he pins me tight again, his arm across my collarbone. I bend my neck and bite down into his arm as hard as I can. He's wearing good thick clothes but still he jerks away and curses. He cuffs the side of my head and I stumble to the ground. He hauls me to my feet again. "Stand still and be quiet," he says. "If you do that again you won't be standing up again in a hurry."

"Please don't touch me," I say. I try to keep the tears out of my voice but I can hear them trembling on my lips.

"Oh shush," he says. "As if anyone would want you for *that,* the way you look. And smell," he adds, with distaste.

Warmth steals over me. I look down to see he is draping a knee-length waistcoat over my shoulders. It's velvet, a finer thing than I've ever worn, embroidered with little flowers, split to panels over my hips. A rich woman would wear a pretty, full skirt under this and a gauzy-sleeved shirt. My stained trousers peep out from the bottom, spoiling the effect. Over the top of this he adds a thick sheepskin jacket, warming me further. It's growing dark now and there are few people left to see the young man with his well-clad wife as they leave the main market square and make their way slowly towards a pair of horses, tethered in the far corner, close to a narrow street. A lantern shines nearby but its flame is flickering, about to burn out.

Now the man turns me towards him. He's tall. I only reach his shoulder and have to tilt my head up to look at him. Broad-shouldered, with wide cheekbones, red-brown skin from a summer of sun and thick dark hair, he's a local. His mouth is wide while his nose is a little askew. His eyes are large and dark. He's looking at me as though I were a ghost.

Keeping his hands firmly on my shoulders so that I can't move he turns my face towards the lantern and peers into my eyes, then over every part of my face, as though looking for something. I stand rigid, waiting for him to throw me to the floor. What else would a man grab a girl for? I try not to shake but I am so afraid. I should have made my home with the brothel owner. At least I would have known what was coming and there might have been someone nearby to watch out for me if a man were too rough. Now I am alone with this stranger and no one will protect me from whatever he wants to do with me. My eyes begin to fill with tears.

He notices. His eyes come back to meet mine and he pulls away from my face a little, stopping his close scrutiny. He loosens his grip on my shoulder and his voice is soft when he speaks. "I am going to put you on this horse. I will take the other. Can you ride?"

I look down and slowly shake my head. Ride? Where is he taking me?

He nods. "Good. Then you won't be tempted to ride off without me, will you?"

He lifts me up onto the closest horse in one smooth movement, as though I weigh nothing. He fiddles with the saddle, shifting my legs to make me sit better. I sit rigid and wait. If I move quickly enough I can dismount and run into the alleyways while he is busy with his own horse. As soon as he turns away to mount I throw myself forward, yanking my legs upwards to get out of the saddle.

I find myself dangling headfirst, my face a hand's breadth from the ground. He bound my legs to the saddle's straps while he was adjusting my seat.

The man gets down from his horse and helps me back up. He doesn't speak until he's back in his own saddle. Then he looks over his shoulder at me. "Your horse will follow mine," he says, and urges his horse forward.

I almost lose my balance as we move.

"Keep your legs tighter together," he advises. "You don't want to fall from that height. And hold the reins, don't just let them drape over her neck like that. Stop holding her mane. Sit up straight."

I let out a little whimper as I let go of her mane and clutch at the reins and he nods with satisfaction.

"Doesn't take much to stop your cheekiness, does it? Now come on, do as I say, you'll have a better journey if you learn to ride a little at least." He narrows his eyes when he sees my hands, so tight on the reins that the horse's neck is pulled down, her chin against her breastbone. "Try not to yank on her mouth like that with the reins, she'll think you want her to stop. We've got a long way to go so you'd better learn fast."

I'm not sure how far we've ridden.

It's dark out here. It must be a few hours since we left the city walls behind us. I could smell the sweet ripe scent of the grapes and the mustiness of the overripe melons, rotting at the sides of the fields outside the city. We headed out east, towards the desert, I suppose, although no one heads straight for that, they go round it, so maybe I'm just confused. I'm tired and scared, although I still can't think what this man would want with me that he couldn't have had in Kashgar or immediately outside the city walls.

As we rode out of the walls I sat rigid on the horse, waiting for him to throw me to the ground and rape me, or kill me – though why he'd want to take my life I've no idea. I thought of calling out to him to ask him why he'd taken me but I was too afraid of the answer. Has he taken me for a slave girl? My shoulders slump at the thought. It seems the most likely reason. A life of drudgery and beatings awaits me, then, with perhaps the odd rough fumble when the mood takes him. My shoulders tense again as another thought occurs. Perhaps he is only a servant and his master has told him to bring a girl to him, one no one will miss, with whom he can – can do as he wishes? I try to stop thinking, my hands are shaking too hard and my lips are trembling with the approach of more tears. I try to think of anyone who will miss me in the market – but why would they? Who would miss a scruffy street girl – and if they did, if they briefly wondered where I was, they wouldn't come looking for me. No one cares what happens to me.

I am alone.

My horse suddenly stops, pushing her nose up against her companion's backside. The man has pulled up without warning and now he is dismounting. "We'll stop here," he announces.

I look around. It's thick darkness now. I can barely see his outline. I'd hoped we might go to a village or even a city, somewhere I could slip away from him. But this is nowhere. Why would we stop here? He approaches and I feel rather than see him untie my legs. Then he offers a hand to help me down. I don't take it. My hands are shaking but I don't want him to see how scared I am.

"Where's 'here'?" I ask, stalling for time.

"Part of the way there."

My fear makes me angry. "And where exactly is 'there'?" I ask.

"You will see when we arrive. Do you wish to eat or not?"

I climb down ungracefully, ignoring his guidance and nearly falling on the ground as a result.

"Make yourself useful," he says. "Pick up some kindling and wood."

I'm about to ask where from but stumble on a stick. I almost have to feel my way around the horses and nearby ground but I put together a few sticks and old brushwood, which he uses to start a fire.

He lifts down his saddlebags and squats beside them, reaches in and takes out some cold hard *naan* breads and a big yellow melon, a long oval in shape, heavy with seeds and thirst-quenching, tongue-tempting flesh. I love these fruits. They're from Hami, where the best melons grow. I've only had them occasionally, the odd bruised slice given as a kindness from a stallholder. He sets it on the ground and rummages about again, emerging with a wrapped up package, bloodied on the outside. Inside are thick chunks of fat lamb. I swallow as saliva rises in my mouth at the thought of it. I rarely eat meat. A doddery old *naan* vendor might not chase you far; a seller of richly spiced skewers of roasted meats most certainly would – and your ears would be ringing if he caught you.

He roasts chunks of lamb over the hot flames and warms the *naans* so that they soften up and taste fresh again. He slices the melon into crescent moons of pale golden sweetness. When the meat is spitting hot he tosses a *naan* to me and I hold it like a bowl, into which he lets fall chunks of the rich meat as it slides off the skewer on which it cooked.

I eat with both hands, taking unfeasibly large bites of the parcelled up bread and lamb, which I nevertheless manage to cram into my mouth. I finish one *naan* in moments and am given another and then still one more. The man raises his eyebrows but I ignore him, my eyes on the food. Whatever this man intends to do with me, he is at least feeding me and I know better than to turn down food. If I am to get away from him, I will be stronger and think better for having eaten well. When my belly aches with fullness I turn to the melon slices, heaped up so that only their skins touch the bare earth. The flesh is juicy-ripe and I eat more than my fair share, slurping at it till my chin is wet and sticky. The man watches me. He's eaten some of the bread and lamb, but not much.

"You'll have to learn better manners than that," he remarks, passing me the melon slices that should have been his share. I devour them and scrape the rinds with my teeth until not one bit of the sweet flesh is left.

The food has given me some courage. Perhaps he won't be a harsh master. I have never eaten a meal as good as this one. "Why do I need good manners? They just slow you down so you get less to eat."

"There will be enough to eat," he says, but his voice sounds odd when he says it.

"Where?"

He doesn't answer the question. He just looks at me. "How long have you been without a home?"

I frown at him while thinking quickly. I must make him think that people will be out looking for me. "What are you talking about? I live in Kashgar with my grandmother. My mother is a sickly sort, so she doesn't go out much. The two of them sit there all day cracking nuts and munching on raisins; the shells everywhere drive me mad. And the gossiping! So I spend most of my time outdoors. I'm to get married soon, though, so I suppose my husband won't fancy me going off here there and everywhere without so much as a by-your-leave. I expect I shall have to stay at home a bit more and mind some babies."

He shakes his head slowly.

"What?"

"Not what I heard."

My lies haven't fooled him. My voice was too light, too unconcerned. "What did you hear, then?"

He tilts his head, looks at the fire instead of me. He sounds like he's reciting a lesson. "You're fifteen. Your name is Hidligh. Old-fashioned name, from before we were Muslims here. Means fragrance. Your mother came from a poor peasant family near the city of Turpan. Your father was a young merchant from Kashgar. Met your mother on a market day in Turpan. Besotted with each other. Good match for your mother, of course, not quite so good for your father. His mother was a widow and she objected to the match. He was always travelling so your mother came to live in Kashgar, in the family home, much against your grandmother's wishes. Treated her poorly when your father wasn't there, fussed over her when he was. Local people felt sorry for her but no one did anything."

He stops and looks over at me. "Right so far?"

I think of this morning, of Mut's lazy son calling after me about the person who was trying to find me. I should have listened to him, should have been more careful. This man knows too much about me. "I wasn't there. Before my time."

He nods. "Your mother fell pregnant, your grandmother became more reconciled. Hoped for a grandson." He stirs the coals. "Cold winter. Your father got sick travelling in the cold and rain, the snow, the winds. Died. Your mother was devastated; his mother nearly went mad. Went to every fortune-teller in town and they all promised the same thing. A boy, yes, of course, a grandson to replace her son. They saw daggers, a palace, horses, power. A boy for sure."

I look up and meet his gaze. I have to brazen this out, make him doubt what he's heard. I cross my arms. "Do I look like a boy to you?"

He shakes his head with a small smile. "A boy with plaits?"

I make a face at him but he's not watching me, he's staring into the flames.

"So: the big day came, your mother had the baby – and it was a girl. Any care your grandmother was taking of her vanished. She dismissed the servants and turned your mother into a maid. She ranted at her day and night, how she'd brought nothing but shame and bad luck to the family, killed off its only living son and turned what should have been a boy to a girl in her womb out of spite." He stops, falls silent.

My earliest memories are of scrubbing floors. My hands were too small to hold a scrubbing brush properly in one hand so I had to use both. Sometimes the brush would run away from me and I'd lose my balance and fall forwards. A floor that needs scrubbing seems endless when you are very small. My mother died eventually, coughing and coughing while I scrubbed and scrubbed. Not long after that I stole a bunch of grapes at the market, too tiny to be noticed as my hand crept over the edge of the stall. When no one saw me and I knew I had been fed better that day than any other since I was at my mother's breast, I ran away and took up my life on the streets of Kashgar.

He stands, stamps out the few remaining coals so they won't start a fire while we sleep, then repeats his first question. "So, how long have you been without a home?"

He knows the answer anyway, no use in lying. "Always."

"What happened to your grandmother?"

I look up at the outline of his shape, faceless in the dark. "You must know that if you know everything else about me."

"She died a few years later. There were some things missing from the house on the day of the funeral."

When I heard the wrinkled old bag was dying I went back to the house and took everything that might be useful to me, mostly clothes which were too large but were warmer than my tight and shredded rags, plus a few coins I found and a small threadbare velvet pouch which I tied round my neck under my clothes to keep money in. Not that I ever had any for long. That was my whole inheritance. I heard her ranting in her room and stood in the doorway. She saw me, thought I was a ghost. Afraid, she told me she never meant to drive me away. When I came closer to take her hand, feeling sorry for her all alone in that empty house, she felt my cold little hands, saw I was flesh and blood. She spat then and cursed me, told me I'd get nothing when she died. Her house had been promised to some distant relatives who had sons. *I dropped her hand and left her there. Four days later I heard she was dead.*

I sit in silence, remembering the smell of dust and her ranting echo in empty rooms.

He throws me a blanket that smells of horse. I wrap it round myself and lie down. The blanket's thick but I grow cold as he walks closer and stands over me. I suppose he'll take what he wants now. I wait. My teeth and fists are clenched. I know it will hurt.

"Got a lot of riding to do," he says. "So get some sleep." He turns and walks away, takes a blanket and settles himself a little way off.

I lie in the darkness. Slowly I unclench my fists but my hands start trembling, so I ball them up again. When I'm sure he won't touch me I finally risk asking what I really want to know. "Why did you bother finding out all that about me? What do you want with me?"

He doesn't answer.

I wait until I'm sure he is asleep. He knows a lot about me, but there's one thing he doesn't seem to have realised. My poor posture, whimpers and clutching at the horse's mane have fooled him.

I'm a good rider. I've worked with horses since I took to the streets. Scraped their hooves clean and brushed them down, held them for rich merchants and fed and watered them for everyone from farmers to noblemen. Sometimes all the thanks I got was the muddy impression of their fat master's boot in my hand from helping them to mount. I got used to them, though, was unafraid even when I was so small they towered over me. When no one was looking I'd hoist myself onto their backs, even when it meant climbing up a wall to reach them. I'd sit there, feeling their warmth seep into my cold body, whispering to them. Later I'd have them walk a bit, when my legs were long enough for my commands to get their attention. A few times, out in the fields away from the main city, I'd find horses pasturing and learnt what it was to ride at a full gallop, terrified by the speed the first few times but always wanting more, till a farmer would inevitably notice his horse galloping around the field with a girl on its back. I got yelled at plenty of times and got a beating twice, but it didn't put me off. So here I am, a poor girl, who should never have been on a fine horse in her life, and I can ride.

My horse is fast but it's not long before I hear hoofbeats behind me, and although I urge her on I know she can feel my defeat because she's not really trying. If he caught up with us that quickly when I had a good head start then there's not much hope. I slow her down and finally stop, then sit there waiting in the darkness for him to reach me.

I wait for him to pull me down from the horse and beat me but he just pulls up alongside. He leans towards me without dismounting and takes the horse's bridle. His voice is flat. "You're going to be hard work," he says, and turns both horses back the way we came. Now he knows I can ride we go faster.

I try not to wonder why he needs us to hurry. The possibilities frighten me.

We ride the next day and night too. I've never been on a horse this long and I'm tired of the jolting and the ache in my thighs. We stop a couple of times. Walking when you've been on horseback for hours is agony: I stagger when I dismount and then hobble like a wounded duck to relieve myself behind bushes. The food runs out and now all I am given is a handful of raisins. Here, in a scrubland far away from any landmark except the odd blackened stump of a dead poplar, with no idea of a destination, there's something gritty and wan about them, as though they need the noise and hustle of a market to give them their true flavour.

It's dawn and I'm drooping over the neck of my horse, half-awake, when at last we stop again. We're in the most barren place I've ever seen. Rocks, sand, rocks, sand, some more rocks and more sand. A huge old dead poplar tree, its bark shredding away. Its branches are decorated with tiny scraps of cloths, tied as symbols of past wishes made. Probably wishes to escape death in the desert. Nothing else. There are sand dunes in the distance but my eyes must be not working properly through lack of sleep, because they're taller than houses, many many houses stacked on top of each other.

I think this madman has actually brought us into the Taklamakan Desert. Any thoughts I might have had of trying to escape from him again fade away. No one can survive out here alone.

We're going to die for sure.

"Here we are," the man says. He dismounts and approaches my horse, then stands for a moment, looking up at me, his eyes tired and somehow sad.

I'm wary. "Where are we?"

"Home."

"Live under a rock, do you?" I ask. I try to sound sharp but my voice comes out shaky.

He doesn't laugh. "Get down," he says. "That's home." He points.

I was mistaken. Rocks, sand, rocks, sand – and a house. It's only one storey high, built low and broad, quite big. Sand has piled up on one side almost as far as the flat roof, and it's made of earth so your eye passes over it thinking it's just a strange shape for a dune. I can only see two windows and they're quite small. It must be dark in there.

I look back at the man and he's watching me. "Is it what you expected?"

I don't know. I don't know what I was expecting. I think I'd stopped expecting anything. "You live here?"

"Yes."

I stare at him, eyelids aching, hands trembling, for once unable to come up with a quick-witted response. "Why?"

It's the only thing that comes to mind. Why would someone with the money for clothes and food and horses live here? No one lives here. They struggle through here only if they get lost, mostly they take their goods along the well-worn trading routes no matter how long the detour, doing their very best to avoid this place.

He takes hold of my reins, turns the horse and then lifts up his hands to me. "Get down."

I almost fall off the horse into his outstretched arms.

Your Free Book

The city of Kairouan in Tunisia, 1020. Hela has powers too strong for a child – both to feel the pain of those around her and to heal them. But when she is given a mysterious cup by a slave woman, its powers overtake her life, forcing her into a vow she cannot hope to keep. So begins a quartet of historical novels set in Morocco as the Almoravid Dynasty sweeps across Northern Africa and Spain, creating a Muslim Empire that endured for generations.

Download your free copy at
www.melissaaddey.com

For readers

THE *CONSORTS* IS ONE OF four existing and forthcoming books set in the Forbidden City. Characters such as the Emperor Qianlong and his mother, Giuseppe Castiglione, Empress Ula Nara, etc., all feature in each book.

You can also sign up for my Reader's Group on my website, where you can download a free copy of *The Cup*, a novella that begins a series set in Morocco in the 10th century. My Readers receive a monthly newsletter with free and promotional reads and are always the first to hear when I bring out a new book.

www.melissaaddey.com

Biography

I MAINLY WRITE HISTORICAL FICTION AND have completed two series: The Moroccan Empire, set in 11th century Morocco and Spain and The Forbidden City, set in 18th century China. My next series focuses on the 'backstage team' of the Colosseum (Flavian Amphitheatre) set in 80AD in ancient Rome. For more information, visit my website www.melissaaddey.com

I was the 2016 Leverhulme Trust Writer in Residence at the British Library and winner of the 2019 Novel London award. I have a PhD in Creative Writing from the University of Surrey. I enjoy teaching and run regular writing workshops at the British Library and at writing festivals.

I live in London with my husband and two children.

Current and forthcoming books include:

Historical Fiction

China

The Consorts (free on Amazon)
The Fragrant Concubine
The Garden of Perfect Brightness
The Cold Palace

Morocco

The Cup (free on my website)
A String of Silver Beads
None Such as She
Do Not Awaken Love

Ancient Rome

From the Ashes
Beneath the Waves
On Bloodied Ground
The Flight of Birds

Picture Books for Children

Kameko and the Monkey-King

Non-Fiction

The Storytelling Entrepreneur
Merchandise for Authors
The Happy Commuter
100 Things to Do while Breastfeeding

Thanks

Thank you to Joanna Penn and Nick Stephenson (and the 10k FB community) whom I consider my virtual mentors, for massively speeding up my learning process. Thank you to Ryan, who goes way above and beyond being supportive and my children for letting Mamma have a little bit of writing time here and there. Thank you as ever to the Streetlight Graphics team, who let me get on with the writing!

Printed in Great Britain
by Amazon

23181507R00078